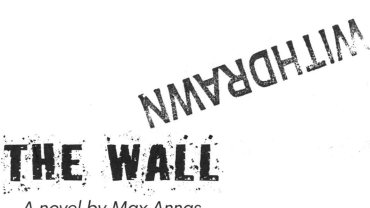

THE WALL

A novel by Max Annas

Catalyst Press

Livermore, California

The translation of this work was supported
by a grant from the Goethe-Institut.

GOETHE
INSTITUT

For further information,
write Catalyst Press,
2941 Kelly Street, Livermore, CA 94551
or email info@catalystpress.org
In North America, this book is distributed by
Consortium Book Sales & Distribution, a division of Ingram.
Phone: 612/746-2600
cbsdinfo@ingramcontent.com
www.cbsd.com

In South Africa, Namibia, and Botswana,
this book is distributed by LAPA Publishers.
Phone: 012/4010700
lapa@lapa.co.za
www.lapa.co.za

FIRST EDITION
10 9 8 7 6 5 4 3 2 1
Library of Congress Control Number: 2018964502
ISBN: 978-1-946395-14-6

Cover design by Karen Vermeulen, Cape Town, South Africa

"White people are weird..."

"What do you mean?"

"Well..." The woman was wearing a faded brown smock covered with large yellow flowers, a light green t-shirt underneath. A dark green skirt peeked out from underneath the smock hem. Sneakers and short black socks below. Her steps were short and quick. "They have no fashion sense," she said. A large artificial leather handbag dangled from her shoulder.

"That's old news." The man glanced down at the woman and swallowed a grin. He was two heads taller than her and was wearing a charcoal-colored suit. "They've never had a clue about that. They're still farmers, at least in their heads. Just look at them." His long legs made it seem like he was taking a leisurely stroll.

"Farmers, yes, that's what they look like," the woman said. With two hurried strides, she reduced the distance she was lagging behind.

"Boy, it's hot!" The man in the suit tugged a handkerchief out of his pants, and dabbed his forehead and cheeks. He wiped the back of his hands as well, before sticking the cloth back in his pocket. "What made you think about that?" He cocked the collar of his light blue shirt and straightened his black tie, an oversized briefcase gripped in his other hand.

The woman ran her arm across her face. "The old man just now."

"Where we parked? The one at the intersection?"

"Uh-huh." The woman nodded. "Baggy shorts, shirt hanging out." She took a couple of long strides to keep from falling behind. "What a shirt! And socks with sandals?" The woman shook her head. "I wouldn't even go to bed in that."

"You don't wear anything to bed."

The woman gave the man a grim look. "Did you see his eyes?"

"Except in the winter..." He grinned. "And just for a second. I didn't want to stare. That would've just made him angrier."

"It's ridiculous. In a day or two, he'll be telling his friends about the two blacks who parked in front of his crappy house. That's what makes me so mad. I mean, what does he think is going to happen to him in the middle of the day? In the suburbs."

"On the hottest day of the year."

"Exactly. On the hottest fucking day of the year. He's more likely to die of a heart attack than a mugging anyway. Even if two blacks did park outside his door. I hope it won't be too hard to find where we left the car later."

"It'll be fine, it's up near the entrance. Somebody's coming."

The woman fell back a few meters, her head now lowered as she walked. Suit lifted his head and studied the woman coming their way. Mid-thirties, business attire, a trim black suit and white blouse. Blonde hair, straight to her shoulders. Realtor type.

"How do you do?" asked Suit, nodding casually.

"Hi," the realtor said, hardly glancing at Suit and ignoring the woman in the smock. "It's a hot one," she said before moving on.

The woman in the smock remained silent, her eyes still fixed on the ground. Once the realtor was a few meters away, she asked: "How far should we go?"

The houses right around here all had two stories, and were built on similarly sized, though differently shaped, plots. They all looked remarkably alike, just like the one-story houses that dominated the streets closer to the entrance.

"We're almost at the end. See the wall over there?"

"Uh-huh. What do you think the old man's got?"

"The old man? The one who stared at us? Pfff...No idea... A little jewelry, two or three generations of gold wedding rings. Cash, maybe even a lot of it. He might be a collector, coins or something. That could be interesting, though it's always hard to get rid of stuff like that. If he has a gun, it won't be anything we could get much for. And no phones that would interest us, no laptop. He definitely owns a CD player, which isn't worth anything these days."

"You have a good eye."

"It's what I do."

"True."

The two of them reached a T-intersection. They could see a tall wall running behind the yards in front of them. Behind it, the steady rush of a river. Barking from over that way. A masculine voice calling to a dog. The man and the woman came to a stop.

"What do you think?" asked Suit.

The gated community was ideal for their purposes. Tons of houses, reasonably sized yards. To create some degree of privacy, walls of varying heights had been built all over the place, functioning as a visible screen against the neighbors and people who walked or drove past. However, none of the walls fully enclosed the yards, which were all freely accessible. And each of those spaces provided opportunities for momentary concealment. As long as you knew where the cameras were.

"The two open windows," the woman commented. "They're not at home."

"How do you know?"

"The car that passed us a few minutes ago pulled out from there."

"The couple?"

"Uh-huh. But it was two men, I think."

"Really? Well, that's the good thing about the heat. They leave their windows open. Did they look as if they'd have something worth taking?"

"Maybe. Not sure."

"What else?"

"The mailbox with the three envelopes sticking out."

"Definitely."

"And then the little dog. The window's shut, but the pane's all smeary. He's waiting for his old lady, his old white lady."

"You think the dog's been left home alone?"

"Yes. What about you?"

"The lights."

The woman shook her head. She hadn't noticed.

"The house with the shrubs by the door," the man said.

"Oh yeah."

"The light just went on, though you almost can't see it. Somebody screwed up the timer."

"But if they have a lighting system and timer, there's got to be an alarm."

"Yes, could be. Probably so. What do you think?"

"First the dog, then the windows. We can see from there."

Suit made a short grunt. "Speaking of dogs," he commented, pointing in front of them. A gaunt, brown dog loped across the narrow street.

"Where'd he come from?" the woman wondered.

"He could've come from anywhere. It's a little like a township around here, dogs running around and all."

"Yes, but the security is tighter than in a township."

"Until now," the man said. "Was tighter."

 "Need a push?" the professor asked.

"I'll be all right," Moses said. "If I'm pointed downhill, it should start just fine. See you tomorrow."

As he released the brake, the old Toyota started rolling. He could still see the professor with his head of curly white hair in the rearview mirror. He waved through the back window before turning around again. Moses gave a quick goodbye honk as he cranked the motor. It choked a couple of times, but then turned over. Bad Kwaito was blaring on the radio. The music broke off for a moment, before starting up again. Something electronic this time.

Huge houses like this annoyed Moses. Most of the time, only a few people lived in them. Like Professor Brinsley and his wife. Two floors, lots of rooms, huge pool, lawn, garden. Fortunately, the prof didn't have any dogs.

It had been a good idea to help Brinsley. His office was stuffed to the ceiling with books sitting on shelves and in dusty piles. His contract with Fort Hare University had run out, and he was flying out for the States next week to start a new job in Atlanta. And the books had to be relocated to the professor's house. Temporary storage.

"Moses, could you use this?" the prof had asked, over and over again.

The Toyota's trunk now contained two heavy boxes of books. And Brinsley had actually parted with C.L.R. James' book about cricket. Unbelievable. His only copy.

An incoming text chimed. Moses pulled his phone out of his pocket.

"Are you heading this way?"

"Yes!" he wrote back.

The next text was right on its heels. "What should we do?"

"Sex!" he typed, his eyes darting from the screen to the road.

He swerved into the oncoming lane as he typed. So what. The street was always empty around noon.

Moses rolled down the passenger window.

"Whoa, whoa, whoa," the DJ shouted. "This is the hottest February in years. And today's the hottest day in the hottest February in years. I'm about to crawl into an ice bath. Call and tell me how you're fighting the heat in the Eastern Cape."

The station cut out, and when it came back, the music had switched to R&B. To the mall to buy prosecco. Then home to change out of these dirty clothes, shower, put on something nice but easy to take right back off again. And finally to Sandi's. Forty minutes max. He would be at her place by one o'clock on the dot.

The phone went off again. It was the battery this time. Almost empty. Oh well.

He was in the curve heading toward Abbotsford when the engine gave a cough. *Come on*, Moses thought. Just one more day. I'll take you to the shop tomorrow. Cross my heart.

To the other side of Abbotsford, then across the Nahoon, almost to Dorchester Heights. The engine spluttered again. *Tomorrow*, Moses thought.

"Tomorrow!" he hollered. It hiccupped back to life. "Come on!" he yelled.

The car stalled again. He was heading down a slight rise, but despite the downhill incline, the motor didn't turn over again. Moses pumped the gas pedal repeatedly.

The road leveled off, and his speed dropped. Moses let the car roll to a stop, making sure to get two of his tires off the pavement. Turned the key and heard... nothing. Pulled out the key, took a deep breath. Stuck it back into the ignition, turned. Silence.

One more time. Removed the key, tried to think about something else, but what? Sex with Sandi. Back in and turn. No response, not even a rattle. Nothing.

The clock. Twelve of the forty minutes were already gone. Moses got out. There were practically no shadows since the sun had reached its zenith. His phone reminded him about the battery. Who should he call?

Khanyo. He knew cars.

"Yeah. Who's this?"

"Moses. The Toyota's died."

"So?"

"So I really need some help."

"Nobody's gonna steal that thing. Where are you anyway? You sound so scared you've got to be in Duncan Village, surrounded by a group of knife-wielding tsotsis. Hahaha..."

Moses laughed, but only because Khanyo expected him to. "Hahaha. I'm in... on the edge of Dorchester Heights. Abbotsford side. Some intersection where a road veers a little uphill to the left. I'm stuck, and I just don't want to be here too long. Listen, if you'll pick me up, you can come over for dinner. I'll cook and fill you in on what Brinsley's said about his successor. Okay?"

No answer.

"Khanyo?" Moses looked at his phone. The screen was dark. Shit.

12:39. Nineteen of the forty minutes were gone. He should go ahead and forget about having sex with Sandi. What had

Khanyo heard? Dorchester Heights? Had he at least heard those two words? And if so, was he on his way?

Moses scanned the area. Suburbia. Upper middle class. Three meters of grass between road and wall, one-story houses, two-car garages, glass shards or electricity running along the wall to keep out the ne'er-do-wells. Further down the road, a gate swung open, and a compact car drove out. Turned in his direction. The woman was thirty, maybe a little older, shoulder-length brown hair. *Housewife*, he thought. *On her way to the kindergarten.*

What lousy luck. Car broken down and phone dead. And dressed the way he was. Ripped pants, covered in dust, oil on his t-shirt from the prof's old bakkie. Moses opened his trunk and rummaged around in the boxes and plastic bags. Where were the clothes he had wanted to give his sister? For the school in the Ciskei. Had he already dropped them off?

He slammed the trunk. Looked around again, remembering something.

He recognized the corner up there. But why?

The road heading uphill. The tall wall. The dead-end road. It all looked familiar. Moses walked slowly up the hill, trying to recall.

Last year. A couple of classmates. They had worked on something together, and the young white man had lived here. They had gotten together at his house. What had his name been? Robbie? No. Janie? No. But something like that. Moses approached the gate in the wall. A large metal sign hanging next to the entrance read "The Pines." Stylized trees rooted beside the letters. The metal gate was just starting to open, a car grill visible on the other side. Moses waited. Brand new. Large. Black. Moses didn't know much about car companies, but he wanted something like that. *Cars like that don't break down on you*, he thought.

The gate was open. The car drove out. Tinted windows. Passed him. The gate began to slowly swing shut. Moses ran forward a few steps and just barely squeezed through the narrow gap before the gated community locked itself back down.

3 "They probably won't be gone long," Suit said. "We should've started with this one."

His eyes traveled up the one-story house with attached garage. Wooden front door, window to the right, tilted open. Two to the left, one of which was also open.

"But the other house had the better location, Thembinkosi. And it was worth the trouble. It would've taken us too long if we'd done things in a different order." The woman glanced around. "Too many sidewalks, too many eyes, that's what you always say. Do you want to go in or not?"

"Yes, Nozipho. We've only just begun to work." He grinned at her.

"They probably don't have an alarm, or they wouldn't have the windows open."

"How many cameras have you counted right around here?" Thembinkosi reached into his pants pocket and pulled out a small bundle of tools.

Nozipho extracted a hand mirror, held it up to her face, and turned slowly, looking in all directions. "I see four of them."

"Me too. That's about right. There won't be many more than that anyway."

Before Nozipho could even fish her lipstick out of her bag, she heard the door click open.

 The metallic clang of the gate was still echoing in Moses' head as he started to question his decision. They all looked the same, these gated communities. Houses facing each other, curving or angular streets, walls on the distant horizon. But he really thought he remembered this place. The six streets that curved away in identical arcs from the wall at the entrance. The houses carefully placed so they didn't sit directly across from each other. The gently sloping site. To the right, beyond the outer wall, a hilly terrain, quite high at certain points. To the left, the road along which he had just come. Moses had a good visual memory. Yes, this was the subdivision he had visited last year. But where did that classmate live? Danie? Or Janie after all? And what would be the best way for him to try to find him?

Three of the streets started to his right, three to his left, all of them running in similarly soft continuous curves to the left. The houses within sight of the entrance were all one-storied. He could see the two-storied ones starting much further back in the enclave. And behind those flowed the river, if he recalled rightly. The Nahoon River, beyond the back wall. He hadn't gone back that far last time. Or had he? But how far was that?

"Remember," Moses said to himself. He walked a few meters to the left and stared down one of the streets, then in the other direction. Decided to start with the rightmost street, tackle things systematically. He'd remember when he saw the house.

How had they actually gotten here last year? Definitely not in his car since he hadn't owned one at that point. He hadn't saved up enough to buy the Toyota until a few months ago. Had they taken Ross's car? Who else had been along? And why in the world was he asking himself these things in the first place?

Because the whole picture would help stimulate his memory. If he could recall the group, their faces, the car, then he'd more easily recognize the house they had visited. And the name would come back to him. Japie? *The Boers have such strange names*, Moses thought.

A symbolic stretch of wall along the street, a few meters of grass and garden, a half-cube with windows, attached garage. Trees that offered a little shade, but were only half-grown. An old Hyundai was sitting in the driveway, two flat tires. Nobody had driven it anywhere lately. The scent of grilled meat, from where? Laundry on a drying rack in the front yard. Who would be home at this hour? The domestic workers, of course. But who else would be inside these walls this time of day? Everyone around here had jobs. And was Japie at home? Or Janie? What had he even looked like? Moses stopped and concentrated. Tall. Thin. Arrogant. Hairline already receding. Talked a blue streak. Moses had taken an instant disliking to him. Oh well, he'd help him either way.

A woman in a smock stood at a window, ironing, her back turned to the window as her massive arms moved slowly across the ironing board. She reached for a piece of cloth and wiped it across her face. The heat. And she was ironing as well. As she finished with the cloth, she turned around and caught sight of Moses. Was startled to see him just standing there, looking in the window. He walked on without waving, rubbed his hand over his sweaty forehead. He glanced at his watch. Exactly one o'clock. The plan had been to be making out with Sandi by this point.

He approached a T-intersection, the end of the first street. As he walked along, he became increasingly certain that his classmate didn't live in one of these one-storied houses. Veering off to the right, another street continued in the exact same curve. Everything still on one level. Moses picked up his pace. Another T. The next street was straight, forking this time slightly toward the left. Running between two-storied houses now. The lots weren't all that large down this street either, the second floors extending over the two-car garages. Flowers were growing in the front yard of one of the houses on the left side of the street. A small bed, every color imaginable. Moses had no idea what kind of flowers these were, but the fact that they were blooming brightly under the brutal sun indicated the amount of work that was being invested in them. He looked around. Who took care of the gardens here? Was there a crew for the entire gated community? Or did each house hire its own gardener? He had no idea how these people lived.

Moses came to a stop a few minutes later and did a double take. There was the house. He remembered the mailbox mounted on a wooden post next to the front door. The box looked like a miniature house open on one side. The wooden roof that extended beyond the two walls protected the box's opening from the rain. Moses took a few steps toward the house, hesitated. Looked more closely. Wrong. This couldn't be it. A Kaizer Chiefs jersey was hanging in one of the upstairs windows. The Boers didn't watch soccer. Ever.

And Japie or Janie or Danie was a typical Boer boy. Moses would have picked up on anything out of the ordinary. He shook his head. Kaizer Chiefs fan. Downright subversive. This wasn't the house.

He paused again at the next T, glancing all around him. He had now covered most of the distance to the wall running along the river, almost the full length of The Pines. He took a couple of steps down the next street before realizing that something had caught his attention as he'd scanned the area. He looked back at the intersection and then up.

A small camera was mounted on one of the lamp posts.

5 Meli breathed in and out. He then inhaled the hot air one more time before turning on the lawn mower. The few blades of grass that were left for him to cut would make it hard for him to breathe for the rest of the day, but he really couldn't complain. He was a gardener by profession. A good gardener, at that.

The exhaust from the old mower puffed up a Woolworth's bag. It shot upward and hung for a second, suspended in the shimmering air. Meli put on the brake without cutting off the mower, as he tried to catch the empty bag. It deftly eluded his first attempt, but he then jumped up and grabbed it.

He caught sight of a figure at the end of the street who was looking in his direction. A little scruffy, but not completely. Good posture. Head up. An afro like some of the young people were wearing again these days. The figure gave a quick wave. Meli waved back.

Not like the two people he had seen a few minutes ago at

the other end of the street. He had instantly registered that the two of them were up to no good. The one in a suit, the other in a smock. Just like in one of those sitcoms that were always playing on TV. But what was this to him? The people around here might not realize what was going on, but that was their own fault.

The figure had disappeared again.

"What is it, Meli?" Mrs. Viljoen. That voice. Even the question was an order. She managed to drown out the engine as well.

"Nothing, madam," he said just as loudly and clearly.

"Then you should get back to work."

"Right away, madam," he said. He pulled his phone out of the pocket: 1:05. Still almost three hours to go until his day was over.

 Thembinkosi quietly shut the door behind them.

"Everything okay with the lock?" Nozipho asked.

"Yep. Even if someone comes and unlocks it, they won't notice anything."

The two of them stood at a window and gazed out. Established practice. First, make sure that nobody has noticed you, then search the house. Usually, time was on their side.

A compact drove past outside.

"I don't like these clothes," Nozipho said.

"But they're helpful."

"You really don't think anybody suspected?"

"Not at all."

"I still don't like the smock. I look like a cleaning lady."

"That was the whole idea!"

"Uh-huh... Do you remember the time we hired that white man?" Nozipho asked. "With the two of us as his servants?"

"Yes, it was a good idea. Too bad the white guy didn't fit the type."

"We bought him those new clothes."

"And he still managed to look like a homeless person."

"He was a homeless person. But it was a good idea."

"It was a fabulous idea." Thembinkosi broke off. "But honestly, he didn't really act like a white man."

"Why do you think that was?"

"What do you know about class differences?"

"Come on. Don't start in on..."

"I think that was our mistake. We hired a poor white man."

"But a rich one wouldn't have done it."

"Exactly. We should have analyzed the situation better. Our mistake."

"Should we go ahead and start?"

7 Were there more cameras? Moses glanced around. Not on this street. He retraced his steps a short way. Nothing. A little further. Back to the T. This was the boundary between the one- and two-storied houses. Still nothing. Had anyone seen him? Maybe at the entrance? In the other direction, he saw the back of a man in overalls. Someone working in a garden, out in this heat. The man was too far away to hear him. He was just turning on the mower. Noise. The exhaust blew a plastic bag toward the street. The man parked the mower without shutting off the motor, ran after the bag, and caught it as it spun in the air. His eyes then fell on Moses. The man froze for a second, bag in hand. Moses waved. The man waved back with his empty hand and turned back to the garden. As he himself turned back around, Moses caught sight of the next camera. Only a few meters away. It was small, attached to yet another streetlamp. And it was pointed right at him. This made it two.

Somewhere a car started. In second gear now, faster, the noise was drawing closer. The car was now in view, heading toward him. Moses hunched his shoulders and walked deeper into the subdivision, heading toward the wall at the river. The mid-range car drove past him, an older white woman at the wheel. *Keep on walking, searching.* He reached the last T. The street now ran right and left, parallel to the wall. The houses really did all look the same.

Systematically or instinctively? He should go to the right in order to check out the furthest back corner of the gated community, but he had a feeling he should head in the other direction if he wanted to find the house.

The lots along the wall were wider than the others he'd seen, with lawns and gardens along the front and both sides of the houses. Who was watching the footage from the cameras? And how many had been put up in here anyway? He had already seen two, so there had to be more. He heard hammering coming from one of the houses along the wall. Across the street, a laundry basket was sitting outside an open front door. Sounds from inside, some kind of rattling.

Moses kept walking.

He hadn't seen a security shack at the entrance. Wherever the footage was being viewed, it probably wasn't being done on site here. Was anyone at all watching the footage? He had heard of fake cameras being hung up for appearance's sake, but weren't these a little too subtle for that? Too small? Fakes were supposed to be larger and immediately noticeable.

The next intersection. The street to the left returned to the entrance, the one straight ahead followed the course of the wall. The Nahoon was much louder here. Not a large river, perhaps twenty meters across. Normally not very deep, especially now in the hottest part of the summer. A voice called out something. Beyond the wall. A fisherman maybe.

Wow, Moses stopped. He hadn't been wrong after all. Here was another mailbox that looked like a miniature house, exactly like the other one. These were probably sold in some building supply store. His memory hadn't failed him.

And this was finally the house he'd been trying to find. He was completely sure this time. He remembered those funny red and green curtains. "Brought from Europe!" his classmate had said. He had probably even mentioned the country. Moses walked up to the door, quickly scanned the area around him, and pressed the doorbell. It produced a high-pitched tone that dwindled to a screech. The battery was pretty much shot. Moses waited a few seconds before ringing the bell again. The skewed tone again. This could mean any number of things. The Boers were pretty lazy, generally speaking. The battery might have already spent several weeks on the shopping list, but kept being forgotten. Or the new battery had been bought days ago, but since nobody ever rang the bell, it just hadn't been installed. Anything was possible.

But, Moses thought, *another possibility was that nobody had been living here for some time*.

Focus. If he couldn't get help here, where should he go?

| 8 | The lounge and kitchen formed an elongated L. |

The lounge and kitchen formed an elongated L. The large room this side of the front door took up almost half of the house's footprint. Two bedrooms and a bathroom behind that. At the very least, maybe more than that. Somewhere was the connector to the garage.

"Are you going to do this area?" Thembinkosi asked. "I'll take the small rooms."

Nozipho nodded. Thembinkosi studied the furniture for a few seconds. A living room suite in corduroy with a tiled coffee table. A dusty wine rack, almost empty. CD rack, gigantic TV screen. A photo of a young couple on a console table. He with a beard, she with long curls. Both kind of blonde.

"Are they the ones you saw?" he asked.

Nozipho leaned closer. "I told you I saw two men. Did one of them have a beard? Psh, hard to say. Somehow..."

"I know. Somehow they all look alike."

"White people?"

"Uh-huh..."

Nozipho and Thembinkosi exchanged glances, grinned. Nozipho gave Thembinkosi a quick kiss and vanished into the kitchen.

No books, Thembinkosi thought. Bad sign. Books indicated

expendable income, more cash around, though less jewelry. But there might still be one or two small treasures. He already suspected what he would find in the closets. First and foremost, bad taste.

The first door he opened was to a large bedroom. The bed had been poorly made. On the nightstand, a pink clock on the one side, a small rugby trophy on the other. He didn't care about stuff like this. He would rummage around in Madam's lingerie a little later. He shut the door and turned the knob on the door across the hall. The second bedroom. Unused. That did interest him.

As Thembinkosi stepped over the threshold, he caught a glimpse of a smudge on the doorframe. He bent down to examine it more closely. He wasn't completely sure, and this was a rather dark spot in the hallway... However, his first impression was that he was looking at dried blood.

9 Back out again? What else. Moses retraced his footsteps. What other options did he have? There was no way he'd find help here in the gated community. "Hello, do you happen to know how to fix a car?"

Although... he could ask the gardener. Perhaps he would know of someone, or might at least let him make a phone call if he had some free minutes on his account. He was already back at the intersection where he'd seen the gardener. But what if the failing doorbell really hadn't meant anything? Maybe nobody had gotten around to it yet. It might not be a priority for them. Had he really paid enough attention to verify that there were absolutely no signs that someone was living there? He hadn't been thorough enough. He should have taken a look inside the mailbox. Were the flowers in the front yard dried out? Were there any flowers at all? What if all of that didn't mean anything, and Japie or Janie was about to get home? He could hear the sound of an engine not too far off. That might be him. On a parallel street. *Just one more time,* Moses told himself. One last try to get help there. The gardener was nowhere in sight anyway. He turned around and went back.

Already 1:16. What was Sandi doing? Hopefully, she was at least getting a little worried about him. Half the bottle of prosecco should have been drunk by now. And they should be... He didn't want to think about that.

Back down the street along the wall, then to the left. There was the house. No flowers. The lawn was dry, but then again, it was really hot and had been for weeks. Moses rubbed his forehead and neck, wiping the sweat on his jeans. He couldn't hear the car anymore. The windows weren't all that clean. He pressed his nose against one to see inside.

The kitchen, neat. Nothing striking. The mailbox was empty, except for two ads. A building supply store and a chain drugstore, both fairly new. Somebody had recently picked up the mail.

No Janie. No Japie. Moses turned around. So out of the subdivision after all? What should he do then? Stand out by the road and wait? There weren't many taxis around here, so it could take some time. But it would be one way he could get to a shop. The taxi driver might be able to recommend one. Money wasn't a problem. He had several hundred in his pocket.

Or should he wait until someone stopped to help him? Super idea. He was stuck between Abbotsford and Dorchester Heights, two suburbs where pretty much only whites lived. Sure, they'd be willing to stop to help a young black man.

Walking it was then. That was okay, too.

A white man appeared at the corner he had just rounded. Sturdy, but not stout. Shorts, t-shirt. Looked like a rugby referee. Better not to cross his path. Moses turned in the other direction. He needed to get out of here now and call Sandi. The gate would hopefully open automatically from the inside.

Somebody else was coming from the other direction. Shit, a guard. And another white man. A white man in a security uniform always meant trouble. White trash despair. He looked around. The referee was getting closer, his hand hidden behind his back. The thought that he should run flashed through Moses' mind, he might have even winced a little. After a brief hesitation, the referee flinched back a step. He'd been waiting for something like this. Run or not run? Moses was in better shape than both of them. But where? Where could he run to escape? Did he really need to escape?

He could already make out the grin on the referee's face. Focus. The guard was swinging a club in his hand. The referee now pulled his hand from behind his back. Wow! What was that? A pistol? There was no way he'd use that.

Both of them had slowed down. The referee was still grinning. Thin mustache over his upper lip. The guard looked very, very grim. Bristly short hair, a just-as bristly beard around his chin and mouth. Moses realized that his uniform wasn't actually a uniform, just plain black clothing, shirt and shorts. Both of them would reach him in about twenty meters. There wasn't much time for Moses to make a decision. Fifteen meters now, twelve, ten. Only a few steps remained between him and the two men. As if in agreement, both men slowed down even more. Moses wanted to run, but he hesitated. The men both came to a stop in unison. About five meters away from him, possibly less.

Why do I feel so numb? Moses wondered. He hadn't done anything.

"Are you lost or something?" The referee. What was he dangling in his hand? Wasn't a pistol, but what was it?

"You're a long way from home, boy!" The one with the club.

"What should we do with you now?" The referee.

"Should we teach him a lesson?" The other man swung the club solidly into the palm of his other hand.

"Whoa, whoa..." Moses said, raising both hands in front of his chest as a sign that he meant no harm. "I just wanted to visit a friend. Where's the problem?"

"Hm, a friend." The club was now being tapped rhythmically against the other hand. Thud, thud, thud.

"There's no way somebody like you has a friend in here." The referee.

"Do you think he's the one?" The club now gripped in both hands.

Moses had seen the thing the referee was holding in his hand only once before. It was a taser, operated by electrical shocks. Or something like that. Could knock you out. Or even kill you.

"Okay," he said. "You win. What should I do?" He kept his hands up where they could see them.

"Look at that," the referee said. "The boy knows how to behave himself."

"Yes, as long as he sees no way out!" The one with the club. "Now get on your knees, hands behind your head."

"Okay," Moses said. "Right away."

He tensed his muscles for a moment, braced one foot a few centimeters behind the other. Took a deep breath. And took off. Toward the wall, past one of the houses, and back in the direction from which he had come.

"Hey!" he heard behind him. Followed by the sound of the two men also beginning to run.

For one very brief moment, it occurred to him that he had just made a serious mistake. But what other choice did he have? Bastards.

Moses kept running.

 10 Start with the drawers. Utensils in the first one. Nozipho examined it closely, anyway. People sometimes hid their stuff in the oddest places. Lifted up the utensil tray. Nothing. She noticed that the forks didn't match the knives and the spoons were different from the other pieces. Mixed patterns.

In the next drawer, plastic. Salad servers and soup spoons. Scratched up. Nozipho looked around. She caught sight of plates and bowls through the glass cabinet doors.

Another old, colorful mishmash. These folks were definitely not rich.

However, wealth wasn't one of her criteria. Access was. The open window, the door with a decrepit lock, the decoy instead of the real alarm system. Her morning job with the realtors helped with this. Organizing emails and mail. Sometimes she knew a week in advance where it might be worth taking a look.

The next drawer was empty. The fourth one, too. There were four more, one on top of the other, at the other end of the custom kitchen. She started at the floor. Empty. Then, tablecloths and napkins. Old and faded. She wouldn't find anything here. The third was a junk drawer. Toothpicks, cleaning sponges, a pile of folded rags, two new and two half-burnt candles.

Nozipho ran her hand through the drawer. Wait, here was something. A few bills. From Mozambique, worthless. A ring. Perhaps gold. A pen. A heavy watch. Stuff you'd stick in here if you didn't have a better place for it.

This is what it had looked like at their place when Thembinkosi lost his job. Too much to starve, too little to enjoy life. And the two girls had still been living at home back then. One of them about to graduate. And college was expensive.

When Thembinkosi had told her that as a teenager he'd spent two years breaking into houses, she hadn't believed him at first. The alcohol. And when he had suggested starting back at that, she'd said: "You're crazy!"

But by the following morning, she had asked what he had in mind. Completely sober again. They needed money.

Nozipho opened the last drawer.

Wow, she thought. These people weren't all that poor after all.

---

11 Happiness still hadn't shaken off the previous night's chaos. Her daughter had managed to eat something that disagreed with her, causing her mother to start loudly spouting ever new complaints about food poisoning. To top it off, the baby got riled up by all the turmoil and couldn't stop sobbing. As for Happiness, she had felt increasingly desperate because the hours she needed to sleep were slipping away.

Happiness was tired. Much too tired to be watching these monitors. Nothing ever happened anyway. And it was so hot.

In theory, her duties were quite easy. Six monitors for six gated communities. She was sitting in a small room behind the office out of which the management and sales activities for all six neighborhoods were run. There were varying numbers of cameras in each of these areas. Usually eight, but sometimes ten or twelve. And the pictures changed at ten-second intervals. If something happened, she could select a particular camera. A simple keyboard combination. She could also simultaneously watch four cameras on a single monitor. However, when that occurred, she couldn't observe what was happening on the other monitors. She only did that if something really wasn't right somewhere. Last week, she had split one of the computer's monitors when she noticed that a car had been driving up and down the streets in a gated community in Beacon Bay. She couldn't see who was sitting in the car, but she had figured out that it was a Golf. A new model. Golfs were popular among some tsotsis. After a while, the car had driven back to the entrance. The gate had opened automatically, and the episode had ended. Happiness had called Warren, the head of security for the company that managed the gated communities. He had printed out a picture of the car and then disappeared. Happiness didn't know what he did with it.

"You should have told me about that car earlier," Warren had said the following day.

The tabletop fan blew a breeze across her face, but

Happiness couldn't shake off the heat in this windowless space. And she had just caught herself dozing off again. She was a little worried about the boy stalking around The Pines. She couldn't place him. He seemed slightly scruffy, and he was looking at the houses in a way she couldn't understand. Warren was out somewhere, so she couldn't ask him.

She had three options.

She could notify someone in The Pines. There was a caretaker there, a man who ran around in shorts even in the winter.

Warren had said, "Call him if there are any minor problems."

"What counts as minor problems?" she'd asked.

"If someone's hanging around, or something looks funny."

For bigger problems, she was supposed to notify Central Alert. That was the company she worked for. The only reason she was sitting in this room was because the company for which Warren was head of security had a contract with Central Alert.

"What are bigger problems?" Happiness had asked.

"When you see a tsotsi," Warren had said. "Or when you see someone who doesn't belong there."

But who didn't belong there? Warren's answer to this question would be different than hers, that much she knew. And the young van Lange, her Central Alert supervisor, had instructed her to not notify their people about every little thing. "If you think the caretaker can take care of the problem, give him a call."

And then, there were the real problems. In those cases, she should call the police. When an actual crime took place, like if she saw someone break into a house. When that happened, though, there were two other problems. If someone actually broke in somewhere, then that meant she had overlooked something earlier. And most of the time, the police didn't show up anyway.

What should she do about the boy? Happiness was so tired. And it was only a little after one. Still almost five hours until the end of her shift.

12 The second bedroom wasn't very big. One bed, barely large enough for two, with the headboard against the wall. Across from it, a built-in wardrobe in pale wood. A nightstand between the bed and window, a table and two chairs in the corner, near the door in which Thembinkosi was standing. Blue carpet. Cheap furnishings.

Nothing indicated that this room had been recently used. Except for the keyring sitting on the bed.

"Hey," he heard Nozipho call. "Look at this."

He glanced up from where he stood. Nozipho was standing there, clutching a bundle of money. She was having trouble not dropping the bills on the floor. A few of them had already slipped through her fingers. Thembinkosi liked what he saw.

"It's kinda strange," Nozipho declared as she opened the briefcase and stuffed the bills into it. "Who leaves this kind of cash just sitting around? I mean... so much of it." She walked back into the kitchen. "It was stuck in one of the drawers," she added.

Nozipho was right. Who used cash these days? Who paid with anything but a card at this point? Except for them, but they had a reason for it: they were stealing it. Thembinkosi didn't really want to answer these questions right now.

"We need to hurry," he said as he returned to the small bedroom. Out the window, he saw someone jog past. Pretty fast at that. A young black man.

What he'd just seen didn't really count as jogging, Thembinkosi thought. The boy was running away from something.

An older white man now came running after him. Okay. Not from something. From him.

Stress, Thembinkosi thought. *Stress* wasn't good in their line of work.

He turned back to the room and looked around one last time. If the money had been kept somewhere as open as a kitchen drawer, then he might not need to waste time on the usual hiding spots. Not to speak of the unusual ones. However, he wanted to look anyway.

As he stepped toward the wardrobe, he noticed a small suitcase that had been shoved under the bed. He pulled it out and unzipped it. Jeans, t-shirt, a red dress. No model-like measurements, nothing all that modern. Also, women's underthings, nothing very sexy. A cosmetics bag. A guest, no longer young. At least fifty, he guessed. Probably older.

The wardrobe was completely empty. A thin layer of dust lay on the boards and the hangers. He rapped briefly on the inside walls. Nothing. Went through the room one more time. Ran his hand under the tabletop, without much hope of finding anything concealed there. His thoughts darted back to the little guest room in the house in Gonubie, where they had been last year. Carelessly stored boxes and a few tattered pillows sitting on top of them. Carefully orchestrated disorder. It was the pillows that had tipped him off. He'd immediately sensed that there was something worth getting there. And he'd been right. The family jewelry had been hidden in an old stuffed animal, a hippo. Not much, but valuable items, including two diamond rings. The stuff here was different. He shut the door behind him as he returned to the hallway.

 Moses ran along the wall, behind which he heard the splashing of the Nahoon. And random voices. *I'd give anything to be on the other side of the wall*, he thought. The voices were behind him, too. That had to be the referee and the fake security guy.

Moses had the greatest respect for them. He'd seen enough white losers take their frustration out on the homeless or shoplifters. He paused and looked back. They were still there. He was faster than both of them. That was his advantage. Theirs was that they knew this neighborhood. And there were two of them.

*Although...*he thought. They hadn't exactly exploited this

advantage, otherwise they wouldn't just be chasing him to-gether. Moses curved back to the street which ran a few more meters parallel to the wall and then doubled-back in the direction he'd just run from. He could still hear the voices of the two whites in the distance. He assumed the exterior gate should have a light sensor that would auto-matically open it if anyone got close. So, get out, that and only that. And then disappear. His car was locked. Main goal—to get out of here and find safety.

He was just passing the street where he'd caught sight of the camera when he noticed a car driving toward him. He was still far away from it, but he could tell that it belonged to a security company. Blue and silver. Moses spun around and sprinted down the street with the camera. The gardener was standing with his back toward him and was still—or once again—mowing the lawn. As he dashed by him, he turned around, and for a quick moment, their eyes met.

What was that? Did the gardener want to tell him some-thing? Moses didn't have time. He ran around the next corner, caught sight of a house with lowered sliding shutters, and headed toward it. A large garbage can sat between the wall along the property boundary and the house. He hid behind it.

 Thembinkosi was standing in the larger bedroom, looking around. He lacked ideas, inspiration. He opened a drawer in the wardrobe. Women's underwear. Ran his fingers through the small pile. Dull, also dull. Hmm... Again, dull. And, oh...sexy. Black and pink stripes. He imag-ined the slip on Nozipho, and then, him taking it off of her. He stuck the lingerie in his jacket. He had no idea if his wife would actually wear a used slip, but it was definitely hot.

The next drawer held menus. The one on top seemed familiar to him. A restaurant chain that had a branch in East London. He'd eaten there once. Then, a few others he'd never heard of before. Another one whose logo seemed familiar to him. Why did people take restaurant menus home with them?

The large bedroom made a very different impression than the small one. It was stuffed with an oversized bed, two nightstands, a mirrored dresser with a marble top, and three chairs from a suite of furniture whose other pieces had to be stored somewhere else. The coverlet was turquoise. A red runner stretched across the blue carpet. How could you live with all this?

Thembinkosi lifted the mattress and ran his hand underneath it. Raised it a little more and took a look as well. Nothing. He opened the cosmetics packages in the dresser. Two shirts still sealed in their original plastic bags sat in the wardrobe. He checked these out, too. He then left the bedroom and went to the kitchen.

15 The garbage can reeked of rotten fruit and decay. That wasn't the only reason he was thinking about a cigarette. He actually only smoked in the evenings these days, and only when he had a beer in front of him. But a smoke would have been just the thing right now. Moses held his nose and watched the street. The referee was alone when he rounded the corner. They had separated after all. Slow strides. Looking all around. This was Moses' first chance to study him more carefully. He was closer to his late fifties than his early ones. He was wearing a light blue polo shirt over shorts similar to the ones Moses had worn for gym class years ago. His hairy legs were stuck in white socks with a red band at the top, and he was wearing blue and yellow New Balance sneakers.

The referee waved at someone. A car from the security company drove up and came to a stop beside him. Was it the same one he had just run away from? A man in uniform got out, tall and very broad. His smooth, bald head glittered, and in his reflective sunglasses, he looked like a frog. Like a black frog. The two men were less than thirty meters away from him. They were both talking, and the referee was gesturing, as well. Moses could only make out fragments.

"... like a...all of a sudden...young and fast..." The referee.

"...surely soon not far...backup..." The frog nodded.

The referee shook his head emphatically, pointing at his taser. Maybe he was explaining that he hadn't seen a weapon. Or that he'd almost taken him out.

The frog shrugged. The fact that the referee hadn't seen a weapon didn't mean that Moses wasn't armed. Super. The army would show up any minute.

The referee gestured vaguely at the area and walked on. The frog pulled a phone out of his pocket and speed-dialed someone. He leaned against the hood of his car, and started talking into his phone. Moses glanced around. What street would take him closer to the exit?

 A gold ring, a silver pen, a watch that looked expensive but was probably a Chinese knockoff, a handful of Mozambique bills.

"That's it?" Thembinkosi asked. He was inspecting their haul. The gold ring wasn't made of gold after all.

"I went through everything twice," Nozipho confirmed. "At least we have the money."

Thembinkosi pocketed the pen. He left the watch where it was. The Mozambique currency also disappeared into his jacket.

"Uh-oh!" Nozipho said.

"What?"

"They found us."

"That's ridiculous."

"Security's out there."

"Where?"

"Come here!"

Nozipho dragged Thembinkosi to the window by the door. Through the curtains, they could see a massive man sitting on the hood of a small Central Alert car. He was talking on the phone. The silver from the silver-and-blue paint

---

job almost blinded them as it reflected the sun. A logo on the car's door showed a stylized figure in profile. The pistol it was holding in its two outstretched arms was almost as large as its body. Thembinkosi choked back a laugh.

"What is it?" Nozipho asked.

"Look at that idiot. Any township boxer could take him down. Even a flyweight. He can hardly move for all his muscles."

"He doesn't look all that bad." Nozipho glanced up at Thembinkosi. "But what's he doing here?"

"I don't know."

"You don't think he's here because of us?"

"He wouldn't just be sitting there, talking on the phone right in front of us, if he were. Must be something else. A boy ran by a few minutes ago, somebody was chasing him. It must be about him. That guy will be gone in three minutes, tops. Then it's high time we get out of here."

"Are we going in somewhere else?"

"Absolutely not! I don't like the feel around here. Let's go home. Hopefully, the whites haven't stolen our car." He had to grin as he said that.

Nozipho shook her head. She thought Thembinkosi's humor was out of line considering the situation.

 17 The security guy was an idiot. Didn't even take off his sunglasses. Bismarck assumed the other man was staring at his name tag. It was engraved with Bismarck van Vuuren. And then: The Pines, Caretaker. No blacks knew who Bismarck had been anyway.

"Well?" the guy asked.

"We almost had him."

"There's only one?"

"Mmhmm...Like a..." Bismarck fumbled for a word. "But he's young. Twenty. And really fast. The fact he ran off is enough proof."

The man in the sunglasses nodded. "What should we do?"

"We're going to catch him."

"Of course. Sooner or later. I'll call for backup."

"No need. Just wait at the gate. You can cut off his way out."

Head-shaking. "Regulation. If anyone is on the run, I have to call for backup."

"Hm!"

"Who is the other guy back there?" Sunglasses pointed at the next corner.

Bismarck looked back. "Ah...That's Willie. A friend of mine. Helps out some." He waved at Willie. Willie waved back.

"Does he also have one of those?" Sunglasses pointed at the taser.

"Just a club," Bismarck said.

But he knew better. Willie normally had a knife and a small pistol on him. "We have to defend ourselves against them somehow," he always said.

However, no one with Central Alert needed to know that his friend combined his free time with security patrols. Besides, they'd catch the black bastard before the backup got here.

"We'll keep going," Bismarck said.

"You know where to find me." The guard pulled a handkerchief from his pants and rubbed it all over his bald head. He then picked up his phone again.

Bismarck signaled at Willie: You go along there, I'll go here. They would meet up again at some point.

The young guy had simply vanished, but he wouldn't get out. The backup from Central Alert would make sure of that, at least. And after Willie and he actually caught the black, he'd ask once again if he couldn't hire his friend as his assistant. He needed help as it was. The times were getting worse.

"Bismarck!" a shout came from behind him.

A bakkie slowly pulled up. Rob van der Merwe was sitting by himself in the cab. As usual, his crew was sitting on the truck bed.

"Rob!" Bismarck greeted him back. The bakkie stopped beside him. "How long do you need?"

"An hour, maybe two. Are you coming on Saturday? The Boks game. In New Zealand."

"Of course," Bismarck said.

He watched the bakkie drive off. Five people were sitting on the back, four of them in overalls. One not. That was against the rules. He would have to say something to Rob, but it wasn't like he didn't know it already. Considering his experience.

Workers had to always be recognizable as workers. And it was always a good idea to follow the rules.

18 The referee drew closer, peering between the houses and walls. A bakkie slowly rolled up behind him. Moses looked around. He had lost his sense of orientation. The outer wall which could have helped him was nowhere in sight. Now the referee was standing in front of the property where he was hiding.

A black cat padded over and stopped beside him. Watched him without any great enthusiasm. He was neither food nor threat.

"Go on!" he whispered. "Catch some mice!"

Nobody could resist watching animals. He really couldn't use the attention the cat might bring his way. The animal wrinkled its nose, and Moses couldn't tell if that was a reaction to him or the trash in the can behind which he was sitting. It strolled away then.

The referee was talking to the bakkie driver.

Moses crawled down the side yard and came out behind the house. Terrace, a couple of pruned shrubs as separation from the neighboring yard, tomato bushes along the house wall. All the windows he could see were shut. Nothing was moving behind the curtains. He stood up. What he now needed was a plan. Back to the outer wall and then over it. That was a plan.

"As long as he's out there..." Nozipho said, her voice was lowered. Distant. "Man, it's hot in here!" he heard her continue.

Thembinkosi had no idea where his wife was at the moment.

"Of course!" he said. "We'll just wait."

Outside the guard was still sitting on the hood of his Polo. He was nodding, either into the phone or to himself, and wasn't saying anything, or was listening, or was doing both. Thembinkosi wished he could see more of the street, to get a better perspective. Somewhere inside the house, a door slammed heavily. That's right, they hadn't checked out the garage.

The boy he'd seen run past. Was all this about him? He hadn't seen much of him. About twenty, maybe. Fit. What could he have done in here? What had he pulled off that would justify a chase? Was the guard calling for backup?

They had to get out of here somehow. Maybe Nozipho needed to change clothes. There were enough women's clothes in the house. If she looked nice enough, nobody would try to stop her. At least not a black security guy. *He wouldn't dare,* Thembinkosi thought.

 How should you move if you don't want to attract attention? And where were the next cameras?

Moses was back out on a street in the middle of The Pines. It had a slight curve to it, and he could see a fair distance in both directions. Good, if he wanted to see what was going on. Bad, if he wanted to avoid being seen, he thought.

The outer wall was behind the row of houses behind this one. He weighed his options. It was hard to see the wall from the street since it was always at the back end of someone's property line. This was a good thing since he could climb it without being seen by the referee, his wingman, or the security guy. The down side was that anyone stuck in bed sick or skipping out on work today would see him. Someone with a phone. Someone with a weapon.

Moses reached the next T-intersection. Looked around, then to the left and right. Disappeared between a two-storied house and a waist-high wall. A swift survey of the windows, a brief listening for threatening sounds. Nothing.

He was standing at the wall.

He couldn't hear the river from here, since the land rose uphill on the other side of the wall. Moses stood on his tip-toes. With his arms outstretched, he could just reach the upper edge. No protrusions or holes that would make the climb any easier. However, the greatest obstacles were the wires that ran along the top of the wall. Moses counted them. Four all told. He had no idea if he'd feel a twinge if he touched them, or if he'd end up roasted like a chicken in the oven. And there was no way he was going to test it. He just wanted out. Somewhere behind him, the sound of an engine. He looked around, but couldn't see anything from here.

He suddenly recalled a TV show he'd once seen. Not on SABC, probably online, maybe on YouTube. Some kind of scientific experiment in which someone had thrown alumi-num foil over an electric fence in order to disrupt the current. Something from the US. It had been easy to climb over the fence after that. Breaking in for beginners. *Was that realistic?* he wondered. And if so: Where the hell could he get some aluminum foil?

21 Thembinkosi opened the briefcase, adding the ring and pen to the cash and jewelry from the pre-vious house with the little dog. He then shut it and picked it up. The clattering bothered him. He walked back into the larger of the two bedrooms and opened the wardrobe. Shirts you'd wear if you were a farmer. Cargo pants with outer pockets. He shook his head. Nozipho had been right. He took three of the shirts from their hangers. Opened the briefcase again and lay the shirts inside. Shut it again. Picked it up. The clattering was gone. Went back to the front of the house.

He cautiously approached the window. The guard was just standing up from the hood and was waving at someone some distance away. A few seconds later, a second Polo joined the first one. Two men and a woman were sitting inside. The driver rolled down the window to chat with his colleague who'd already been standing there for a while. Then the three new arrivals got out of their car. The driver was in his mid-forties, and he moved as if this wasn't his first rodeo. The other man and the woman were young. Rookies. Glanced around. Had come along to learn something.

Rookies were always bad news. Sense of responsibility, minimal experience, no broader perspective. An unpleasant cocktail that could quickly lead to overzealousness.

"Thembi!" Nozipho called. She was much too loud. He kept his eyes on the four on the street, but none of them seemed to have heard anything. Nozipho only said "Thembi" when she was sexually aroused—or in danger. "Thembi!" she called again.

"Sssshhh!" he said much quieter. "I'm on my way."

"Thembi, come here!" The garage door slammed again with a dull thud. Nozipho stood in front of him, her mouth open.

"What is it?"

Nozipho tried to talk. Failed. Her eyes...Thembinkosi had never seen her eyes like this. What was it? Panic? No... Horror.

"What is it?" he asked again.

Nozipho opened and shut her mouth, but couldn't make a sound. She held out her hand, which was shaking. Thembinkosi took it and let himself be led away. Together they walked down the narrow hallway to a metal door. Nozipho opened it, and they entered the garage. Hardly any breathable air, so stuffy and hot. At the end of a cable, a lightbulb dangled from the ceiling, providing the empty space with a little light. Two or three sunbeams had managed to creep under the door that led outside. The space smelled of engine oil. A shelving unit stood against the wall. Tool boxes. Cooler. Rubber boots. A steel cabinet stood open, almost empty except for two yellow plastic containers. Thembinkosi caught sight of a very large freezer in the corner. That was it.

Nozipho pulled him toward it. She stopped in front of it and stared at the lid.

It took a few seconds for Thembinkosi to realize that he was supposed to raise it. He grabbed the handle and slowly opened the chest.

In the dim light, he could make out the outlines of a human body. He swiftly slammed the freezer shut.

 A tall ladder or aluminum foil? Or some other way out? But how?

Moses returned to the street and glanced around. A mail carrier two corners down was busy doing what he was paid for. Sticking letters in slots. No danger there. Or maybe he'd been informed about everything and was keeping an eye out for him.

If he avoided the main street through the gated community and alternated between the street closest to the wall and the wall itself... Maybe he could reach the exit. Then straight out. First to catch his breath and then to take care of his car.

He thought about Sandi again. It was already after one thirty. She had to be really worried by now. People disappeared every day in South Africa. Just like that. Rarely was this a voluntary decision. Most of them reappeared later— though typically not breathing.

However, before he could be in touch with her, he had to get out of here.

"Hey!" someone behind him yelled. Moses spun around and saw the white man with the club. He took off at once. "Stop!" he heard, but he had already slipped between two houses and was only a few meters away from the outer wall. Keep running. Away from the white guy.

This isn't going to go well, Moses thought as he hurtled over a shrub. Someone would see him. Hopefully, they'd just call the cops and not shoot. He didn't want to imagine that scenario.

The cops, he thought, leaping over a waist-high wall. As he cleared it, he caught one of his shoes on the topmost edge. He briefly struggled to keep his balance, then everything was all right. That wall had been tall. *The cops,* he thought again. Why shouldn't they come to his rescue? He hadn't done anything. Hadn't even thought anything marginally criminal.

Over the next hedge. Lift the one leg high and pull the other one up. And he was lying on his stomach, his right hand under his body. He had tried to catch his fall. Left hand stretched out from his body. Right leg bent, left one extended out where it had gotten tangled in the shrub.

Fortunately, he had fallen on a stretch of grass, but his right hand throbbed. He propped himself up and got to his knees. An alarm siren was going off somewhere. Security? That wasn't a cop siren. As he started to stand up, Moses saw a thin, old woman through the window on the other side of the open terrace door. She was holding a phone to her ear. He took off, clearing the next bush but only with great difficulty.

He couldn't hear the alarm anymore, which had been replaced by the sound of a motor. Not far away. The next wall. Moses leaned forward. As he slowed down, he caught sight of the crack between the window and its sill. He glanced quickly around the yard. Browning grass, beds without flowers, a child's bike, patio table and a couple of chairs scattered about. Everything shut. Terrace door and windows. Only one of them wasn't. He slowly approached the house and looked up at the second floor. The house seemed to be abandoned. Not forever, but just for the day. He carefully raised the window. Children's room.

Think this through, Moses warned himself. *You have to think this through.* The siren momentarily went off again. Close by. Moses jumped up, wedged his body through the opening, and took a deep breath. He then squeezed the rest of the way through and landed head-first on the colorful rug. He quickly stood back up and closed the window. For a moment, he just stood there, listening to nothing except his own breathing.

23 "Luvoyo, the ladder. Peter, grab the materials. Mcebisi, the tools. Fezile, additional supplies. Eddie, you're on watch. Let's go, chaps." Rob van der Merwe clapped his hands. "Hi, Mr. Bartlett," he said more softly. He held his hand out to a fat man wearing a white button-down shirt and light blue shorts. Spots of sweat on his chest and under his arms.

"Hi," Mr. Bartlett said. "How long will it take?"

"Less than two hours. We have to make sure it's tight. That'll take longer than the actual work."

"Friggin' monkeys. I have to go back to work, but for you, this is good business."

"It's okay. It'll take some extra effort on your part, but I always recommend not setting the trash right out at the door. It belongs on the other side of the gate, outside."

"Coffee?"

"Too hot."

"Water? Laziness. Where the trash is concerned."

"That would be great. I know. But that's how you're attracting the monkeys. And if they jump around your roof long enough, you'll need my help. Thank you." Van der Merwe grinned as he took the glass and drained the cold water in a single gulp. "I better go back out and make sure everything's going okay out there. You know how it is. Better to be overly careful."

"Nothing's more important than control. You don't need to tell me that."

Van der Merwe picked a spot where he could keep an eye on his workers. A small thing, really. Just needed to trade out a few shingles. Actually, the entire roof needed to be replaced. But people pushed off stuff like that, preferring to take care of the small repairs while clinging to the hope of being able to postpone the larger investment. Who could blame them in these hard times?

"Don't daydream, Mcebisi!" he shouted. "Get to work. We're getting paid for the work we do, not the time we waste. And don't forget we have to be in Amalinda around 3:30. So..."

He was going to have to have a chat with Mcebisi about coming to work without his overalls. That was the only thing he demanded of them. Never without overalls. And the idiot had also lost the cloth he used to protect his head from the sun. Without it, he'd get sunstroke up there on the roof.

Of course, he also demanded punctuality. And thoroughness. Sometimes it was enough to drive you crazy.

 "What is that?" Thembinkosi asked. Nozipho just looked at him.

"What is that? Why in the world did you even open the freezer?"

"You found 20,000 rand in a freezer once," Nozipho shot back. "Stop with your questions. That's a dead woman."

"Did you look at her?"

"Only a little."

"And?"

"Older than us. White. Not poor."

"White."

"Mmhmm."

"And?"

"And what?"

"What should we do with her?"

"Nothing. We wait until the folks out there leave, and we get lost," Nozipho declared.

"We never should've come in here."

"But you didn't say anything beforehand."

"I know, but I had a bad feeling. And..."

Nozipho opened the freezer again. "We didn't put her in there. We didn't kill her. We simply disappear, and that's that." She lowered the lid.

"How do you know she was killed?" Thembinkosi studied Nozipho.

She gazed back at him. "I don't."

"Then why did you say that?"

Nozipho needed a few seconds to collect her thoughts. "Why would someone stick a woman in a freezer?"

"So she wouldn't smell?"

Nozipho said nothing.

"Because..." Thembinkosi continued. "It is the hottest day of the year?"

Nozipho nodded, looking thoughtful. "But...what did you do when your mother died?"

"Called a doctor."

"But she was dead. Why a doctor?"

"Because...because...I had to do something."

"But you knew she was dead."

"Sure," Thembinkosi said. "I somehow knew that, but maybe part of me wasn't certain."

"And on that day, did it ever occur to you to stick your mother in a freezer?"

"Are you nuts?"

"But it was hot when she died. I remember that."

"But still!"

"See?"

"See what?"

"That people don't stick women in freezers. That's what I wanted to say. Even if they're dead."

"True," Thembinkosi said. "I know that, too. That's just not something you do."

He stared at the floor. He saw a spot in front of the freezer that reminded him of something, but he wasn't sure what.

The light in the garage wasn't bright enough for him to recognize what had dribbled on the gray floor. He pulled his phone out of his pocket, leaned down, and shone a light on the spot. And then he remembered.

He slowly straightened up and opened the chest. The woman looked so peaceful, like only a person lying dead in a freezer possibly could. The light from his phone revealed a slightly wrinkled face, sparse gray hair, a striped t-shirt, and denim shorts covered with appliques.

"Hold the lid," Thembinkosi said before slowly stretching one hand into the freezer. He touched the corpse's knee and quickly yanked back his hand.

"What is it?" Nozipho asked.

"She's still warm!"

25 White dolls. White pop star girls on posters. He didn't recognize any of them. The room was stuffed full of bright things. Yellow sheets, red rug, stuffed animals in every color imaginable. Moses picked up a pink elephant from a shelf, which declared "I love you" in a high-pitched voice when he turned it over. Momentary fear. Had anyone heard that? He set the elephant back down and listened hard once more for any noises in the house. Opened the door to the living room and looked through the terrace door to the outside. That's where he'd just come from. He then walked to the front of the house.

The vehicle whose siren he'd heard was sitting almost right in front of the door, its lights flashing. The guard he'd seen just a little while ago, the frog, was sitting at the wheel and talking to the white man who liked to swing his club so much. The two of them didn't look like the best of friends. Moses couldn't hear what they were talking about, but he could tell that they were only exchanging short sentences. The man in the car nodded curtly, as did the man with the stick. After that, they just stared down the street. What plan had the two of them cooked up?

Did they even have one?

He walked back into the living room in search of the kitchen. Opened the fridge, took out the orange juice, and drank straight out of the bottle. After that, he stuck his head under the faucet.

No aluminum foil in the drawer. Nor in the pantry. Maybe they'd just run out of it. Or it was kept somewhere else.

For the first time, he felt safe, since nobody could see him in here. But how long would this feeling of safety last? Only until the owners returned. Until they started searching the houses.

Moses put the juice back up. No, they wouldn't do that. Private property was sacred in South Africa. Every thief in the government swore by that. The houses would remain untouched for the time being.

Cheap furniture, but expensive appliances. A monstrous flat-screen TV hung on the wall. Speakers large enough to fill a stadium with sound. Two MacBooks on the desk. How careless was that? Sitting next to an old telephone that you couldn't even buy anymore. Moses briefly considered going up to the second floor, but he had other concerns. He crept around the first floor and quickly opened all the doors. The only locked door was a steel one. *The garage*, Moses thought. *The ladder*, an afterthought.

Through a street-side window, he saw the old woman he'd just seen on the phone. She was talking to the two men. Pointed at her house, then at the ground—he was lying in my yard. She gestured to the side—and ran off. Now she shook her head—this country wasn't safe anymore. If she had been alone with the white guard, she would've added that things had been better before. He'd understand what she meant.

An old man walking a small dog on a leash approached them. He kept looking all around as he drew closer.

Moses groaned. Only old people and whites, and old white people, lived here. He thought about the phone.

He went over to the desk and lifted the receiver. A dial

tone. Why hadn't he thought about this right away? He could finally call Sandi.

 26 "What do you mean, she's still warm?"

"Touch her," Thembinkosi said, lifting the freezer lid again.

"No," Nozipho said. "I don't want to. Why is she still warm?"

"Because she hasn't been dead all that long."

"But..."

"And because she hasn't been in the freezer long."

"And..."

"We have to get out of here."

"But...The men in the car must have put her in there."

"Maybe."

"Why maybe? Who else could've done it?"

"I don't know. I'm not here to..." Thembinkosi broke off. He wasn't sure how to end the sentence.

"What?"

"... to investigate a murder."

Nozipho stared at him. "You just said *murder*."

"Come on," Thembinkosi said, taking Nozipho's hand again. He pulled her back into the house and to the door to the smaller bedroom. He opened the door so that more light fell into the hallway. "There!" He pointed at the spot.

"What is that?"

"I think it's blood."

Nozipho leaned down to look at it closely. "And that makes you think the old woman was murdered? Maybe she just cut her foot or something."

"You just said it yourself. What other reason could there be to put her in the freezer instead of calling the doctor or the police?"

27 If only he could remember Sandi's number. The one for the new phone she'd had to get after her old one was stolen on the bus taxi. He'd saved the number on his own phone and then... forgotten it.

Remember. You see her number every time you send her a text. Visualize the number. "082," he muttered to himself. It begins with 0, 8 and 2. Obviously. But then...

Remember. You see this number every day. 082, then... two of the numbers were doubles. That was over half the battle in terms of the seven digits he still needed.

But what could Sandi actually do? Call the police? Surely the others had already done that. The double numbers. Come on! If worse came to worse, Sandi would see him being taken away. And maybe she wouldn't come alone. Witnesses were always good.

Two sevens, and two...two nines. The first pair early in the number. 082, then a 4, then the two 7s. 082-477. The two nines were close to the end. Right?

Or right at the end. That's it. 082-477, then two other numbers followed by the two nines. The old man who'd just shown up began to gesture wildly. He pointed at the little dog, an ugly creature with what looked like a hairbrush at the end of its tail.

Odd numbers. That was it. He had noticed that most of the numbers were odd at some point when he'd been sending a text. Other odd numbers appeared between the sevens and the nines. What was left? A one? No. Three and five? Or five and three?

Moses took a guess. 082-477-3599. Dial tone. Ringing. Waiting. "Hello?" shouted a man's voice. He hung up.

082-477-5399. Another dial tone. Ringing. Waiting.

"Hey!" Sandi said.

"It's me."

"What's up? Why aren't you coming? Why is your phone dead?"

"I can't."

"What do you mean...you can't?"

"I'm stuck."

Moses told her the story from the moment the car rolled to a stop. About Khanyo, about the classmate whose name he couldn't remember, about the referee and the white man with the club, and about running away.

"And where are you now?" Sandi asked after he stopped talking.

"In a house."

"Whose house?"

Moses considered what he could possibly say. Before he could reply, Sandi continued: "You broke in?"

"The window was open."

"Shit. What should I do?"

"I don't know."

"The police."

"No police."

"Well, sure, but what then? Where are you exactly?"

"Between Abbotsford and Dorchester Heights."

"That's the middle of nowhere."

"That's suburbia. It's called The Pines. White people live here, lots of them."

"That much I know. Should I come there?"

"And then what?" Moses asked.

"Where's the house located?"

"No idea. I just ran."

"I'll bring along everyone we know!"

"That's good. Don't leave me here alone!"

"Absolutely not," Sandi agreed. "No way!"

"I love you," Moses said.

"I love you back. Come to the entrance." With that, Sandi hung up.

Something had happened wherever the old man had come from. Moses wondered if he had trampled through his garden, too. Had he crunched his hedge? Tipped over a garden chair? The man rubbed his face, then did it again. The white guy with the club patted his arm and pulled a package of tissues out of his pocket. Handed the man one. He was clearly crying. Shaking her head, the woman who had seen him fall was saying something to the old man.

Because of the hedge? Not hardly. *Maybe this was his chance*, Moses thought. While the others were busy with whatever had happened to the old man, he could escape out back. He walked over to the terrace door and looked through the pane. Straight along the wall as fast as possible. At some point, he had to reach the gate and then freedom. He was about to turn the key in the glass door and open it, when it occurred to him that he might set off an alarm. Some doors and windows were part of the security system, and an alarm would go off if you opened them. That's exactly what he didn't need.

Moses returned to the child's room and opened the window. That hadn't caused any problems earlier and wouldn't now either.

He cautiously stuck his head out, looking right and left. Nothing. He slowly lowered himself through the window until he was back on the terrace. He then kept running in the direction he'd been going. Less panicked. Calmer. He knew what he wanted. He had to somehow reach the exit. And Sandi had to come up with a plan.

28 Hlaudi gazed out of the car at the white guy. He was dressed in all black. Faded short-sleeved shirt with epaulettes. Obviously sewn on. His skinny legs stuck out of wide shorts with thick pockets. His face was haggard. He looked like someone who'd smoked way too much over the years.

"Almost caught him!" the white man said.

Almost caught means didn't catch, Hlaudi thought.

"Doesn't always work out!" he said. "Next time." He barely managed to keep from grinning.

"The bastard was really fast!"

"Young. I saw him running."

"Twenty or so."

"Uh-huh."

Hlaudi watched as the white guy shifted his rubber club from one hand to the other and then back again. He looked like someone who didn't have a job and was doing this for fun. There was no way he could afford a home in here. *How much did they cost in here anyway,* he wondered. Regardless, more than he could afford. Much more.

"Hello!" a voice came from behind them. "Hello!"

In his rearview mirror, Hlaudi watched an old woman in blue pants and a white t-shirt slowly approach them. The white guy beside him propped his hands on his hips, and the woman finally reached the car. She looked back and forth between the two of them before turning to the white man.

"...can't believe it...in front of my door...suddenly...and fell down...ran off..." The white guy kept nodding. The woman once again glanced at one man and then the other. She paused. "Which of you is..."

"He is!" The white guy pointed his club at Hlaudi.

"... responsible?" the woman finished. "Then..."

"The boy ran off?" Hlaudi asked.

"Yes, like I just said," the woman said. Hlaudi could see that she was gradually calming down.

"How did he get in here in the first place?" she asked. "Aren't you supposed to make sure nothing like this happens?" She shook her head so emphatically, Hlaudi was concerned she might sprain something.

"No, we're not," he answered. "But we'll catch him."

More movement in the rearview mirror. This time it was an old white man who was walking up to the car. Brown suit pants, white shirt. Earlier government employee, Hlaudi guessed. Much earlier from when the system had been completely different. Only, he didn't look as relaxed as most whites did when out walking their dogs. He waved at them.

Or only at the white woman. Or at both whites. Or at him perhaps because he was sitting in a security vehicle. Hlaudi couldn't tell.

"Break-in." That was all the man said when he reached them. He had stubby white hair and was gasping for breath. "They were in my house." He pulled a perfectly folded white handkerchief out of his pocket and dabbed his forehead with it.

"Oh no, my dear..." the woman said, placing a hand on his shoulder.

"Nobbie was all alone in the house." He pointed at the dog that Hlaudi could no longer see from where he was sitting in the car. "I noticed right away that something wasn't right." He hesitated, clearly expecting to be asked a question.

"Is anything broken?" Hlaudi asked.

"The lock was funny. I immediately noticed that something wasn't okay with it."

"And what's missing?"

"My money's gone," he said. "And some jewelry."

He started to cry. The white guy with the club handed him a tissue.

 The screech of brakes outside. Thembinkosi and Nozipho walked across to the window in the small bedroom and looked out. Another Central Alert car, again a Polo. Again, two more people who initially stayed inside the car. The car with the guard who had first been there had disappeared. The two drivers of the two remaining cars were talking to each other. The two rookies who had shown up earlier were standing a few meters away, also chatting.

"They'll blame us for it!" Nozipho declared.

"For what?"

"The murder. If that's what it is."

"Did I tell you that I saw a boy running away?" Thembinkosi asked.

Nozipho shook her head. "You think he..."

"No, but that's why they're here."

"And...the woman..."

Thembinkosi glanced around the room again. "Did the

two people in the car really come from here?" He left the room and returned a few minutes later with a photo from the lounge. "Was this one of them?" he asked.

Nozipho took the photo from him. "Well...I don't know."

"But it was two men, right?"

"Uh-huh. Think so. I didn't pay enough attention. I didn't want to stare."

Thembinkosi retrieved the photo, and tried to imagine the bearded man without a beard and then just unshaven. But he couldn't be sure. "I also didn't look at them carefully. Didn't seem important. We have to get out of here."

"But how?"

"You'll need to put on something else. Come on!"

30

Much better to stay calm, Moses thought. He was still sweating like a pig. He also looked like one. The dust from this morning on top of the sweat, falling down in the garden, climbing through the window. All of it had left a mark. And he smelled like a pig, too, he determined.

Over the next hedge and into the next yard. Suddenly, there was a wall jutting out from the outer wall that was too tall to leap over. He came to a stop and saw that the chest-high wall separated two properties. So, he headed toward the street and carefully looked both ways.

The security car was concealed behind the curve, which probably meant the people couldn't see him either. The problem was that he didn't know how far the gate was. He had changed direction so many times, and The Pines was so large that he felt lost. Running along the outer wall seemed to be the safest solution, but it was also the most time-consuming. The numerous obstacles. The undesired contact with the people who were home at this hour. Why not shorten his path? Maybe covering a few meters on the street was the best course of action.

One last question. Run or walk?

Three seconds of consideration. Running shortened the

duration, but it looked suspicious. Walking cost more time, but alarmed fewer people. Moses opted for the slower variation.

He took the street that started across from where he was. A short distance into the subdivision, then turn and see the exit. Walk calmly. Don't look all around. *Stay cool*, he warned himself. *Keep going, just keep going*, he thought. It might all be over soon.

Turn. Keep walking. The street he had started walking down soon ended in the one that ran closest to the outer wall. This offered him the opportunity to quickly disappear behind the outermost houses. This was what he suddenly wanted to do, too, since he was feeling visible. Much too visible.

I shouldn't look around, Moses thought, *but I really want to*. One, two, three. Just to make sure no danger was creeping up on him from behind. He stopped and checked his watch. Almost two o'clock. He then glanced behind him. Shit. It was the white guy from earlier. The one with the club. He was once again slapping it against his palm, and he was rapidly closing the distance between them.

Moses started running again. First, slowly, then faster. Up to the T-junction, by which point he would have to decide to go either right or left. Accelerate. Run even faster.

A car was now rolling toward him. Security. Damn it. Trapped! Moses stopped and looked around. The white guy was still behind him. The car ahead. He vaulted over a few brightly blooming flowers and vanished between two houses.

 Thembinkosi opened the wardrobe in the large bedroom. As he did so, he recalled the slip in his jacket pocket. Better not bring that up right now.

"Well?" Nozipho asked.

"Pick something out."

"But what?"

"Whatever fits. And looks good on you. And you like."

"Hmm...And you think this is the best strategy?"

"Can you think of anything better? The maid get-up is only good as long as no one looks too closely. Now we need something new."

Nozipho pulled a dress out of the closet. Yellow and white pinstripes. Sleeveless. She hung it back up. Another one was red with randomly splattered ochre spots. A plain one in navy.

"What's wrong?" Thembinkosi asked. "They're all nice."

"Don't really fit."

"What do you mean? Too tight?"

Thembinkosi picked one up and examined it. It was black, and the fabric flowed pleasantly through his fingers. Somehow the fashionable dresses didn't fit with the rest of the apartment.

"Obviously too tight."

"Mmhmm...Just keep looking. You'll find something."

When Nozipho didn't reply, he added: "And even if something's a little tight...I like it that way. And the boys out there will, too!"

"Get out now," Nozipho ordered. "I'll figure it out."

 Hedges and walls, waist and shoulder high. For the time being, they were shielding him. Crouched between four houses, Moses saw the ninety-degree angles of the walls. The street he had just come from was behind him, the next one in front of him. This was the one he needed to cross now. And the one he was afraid of.

"The hunt has begun," he muttered quietly.

A voice behind him. "He has to be somewhere."

That was the white man. If he was talking to someone, then the car and whoever was in it had to be behind him as well. And the street in front of him might not be watched yet. So now he had to run. Moses burst through the hedge and caught sight of a barred living room window. To the right or the left past it? Didn't matter.

He veered to the left.

Past the house with another wall along its side, now the front yard. Something was blooming there. He hesitated briefly before reaching the street, then sprinted on.

Quickly checked down the street both ways. The one side of the street was empty. Anything but empty in the other direction. He leaped into the next yard. Rapidly assessed the situation. One story. Blinds down. Good. Unoccupied or empty. Behind the house. Think fast.

The only thing sitting in front of him was the outer wall. What was it he had seen the split second before he had slipped back here? A car, parked, someone standing next to it. Had it been painted blue and silver like the security company vehicles? Yes, probably. So, another car. And the person? What did he remember? A man. No, a woman. How old? Who cared. He couldn't remember all the details. The important thing was the car. Whoever had been sitting inside had seen him. And what would they do now? Drive in the direction that Moses would be heading. Toward the exit.

And so he would do the opposite. Even if it pained him to do so. Back toward the river, in the other direction. In the wrong direction. He kept running. Hedges and walls.

Walls and hedges.

He was now being careful whenever he leaped over them. After taking a few jumps, he knelt down and looked around. He hadn't even noticed that the houses around him were all two-storied again. This wasn't good, since it meant that he had finally reached the back part of the gated community. When all he wanted to do was get out of here.

Moses was crouched on a terrace decorated with an array of flower tubs. Colors splashed everywhere. Plastic table and chairs. Bars on the door and windows. He raised his head over the hedge and looked back.

He caught sight of a uniform back where the one-storied houses were standing. At least he had made the right decision. Running toward the exit would have put him on an intersect course with that man. A second person in uniform joined him. They were talking, coming in his direction. Walking. Far away. No danger.

For now.

He turned around.

In the neighboring yard, a man was standing on the terrace, gazing in his direction. Moses jerked his head down immediately. Scooted a little to the side. The bushes were a little less thick here. Tried to peer through them.

The man was around fifty. Heavyset. Mostly bald on the top. Probably blonde originally. T-shirt with the stupid Sharks logo, the one with the shark running around with a rugby ball. He now turned around and reached back before putting on some glasses. Stared back in his direction. Removed the glasses again. Squinted. Then vanished into his house.

Moses slowly turned around. The two guards were walking toward him, but were still far off. He squeezed through a gap in the hedge into the next yard. On hands and knees. Peeked over a wall that was only knee-high, into the house in which the man had just disappeared. He couldn't see him through the terrace window.

That meant...absolutely nothing. The man might be hiding behind something and watching him, too. But what other choice did Moses have? He scrambled over the little wall and looked through the window once more. Nothing. Crawled on. Took a header over the next wall. Waist high. Landed in a bed. Pain. Moses pulled himself together and rolled on. A thorn was stuck in his lower arm. He pulled it out. Studied the small bush he had just flattened. Some kind of yellow fruit. The guards weren't far now.

Getting closer, and he was caught in a corner formed by the outer wall. Close to the river. Scrambled over another wall and another hedge that he more squashed than cleared. Now he could see around a house corner.

Not far away, perhaps only three yards over, several people were standing and chatting. A guard was with them.

Moses could sense their excitement. Most of them were white, only the guard was black. He really didn't want to know what they were talking about. He wanted out of here. He wanted to get away. But how? Look around!

And Moses couldn't believe what he saw. Shut his eyes and opened them again. It was true. The neighboring terrace door, only a few meters from him, was open a crack. People could be so careless, despite the fact they were so afraid of burglars, of black burglars... But when it came to precautionary measures, the normal ones, they failed miserably. Through the door and into the house. And then catch his breath. Like before. That was the new plan.

Nobody was looking his way. He very slowly pushed apart the hedge and crawled through. Slowly, don't do anything frantically. Only a few more meters. The stretch between the well-manicured yard and the tiled terrace. The open door was almost within reach. Only one more meter.

He had to pull the door open a little, then he was through. Flipped over onto his stomach before sticking his head back out the door to check the situation. No one had noticed him.

Moses stood up and stretched out his back. All this crawling around was demeaning. The running, too.

As well as the hiding. He closed the door quietly and listened inside the house. Nothing. No noise anywhere. Nonetheless, he decided to be very careful. But first he needed something to drink.

33 Thembinkosi watched yet another security vehicle drive up. Now there were two Polos and a brand new Toyota bakkie from which emerged four more people. Five men and two women were now standing in front of the house, all in Central Alert uniforms. The driver of the second Polo looked like he was in charge or, at least, the highest ranking among them. He was talking and gesturing, and then he shrugged quickly. Just wait. He wagged his pointer finger, too. We'll catch him. Someone in the group nodded.

Of course, boss. What else could he say?

"Well?" He heard Nozipho behind him.

He turned around. She was actually wearing the white dress with the yellow pinstripes. It fit after all. She looked great.

"It's a little snug!" she said.

"Doesn't matter," he said, looking her up and down. "The sneakers look a little funny, don't you think?"

"Hmm...Yeah, but I'm keeping my own shoes on. But if I end up having to run, this dress won't just be snug. It'll rip. We're not at that point yet, though. Not yet." She joined him at the window: "What's going on out there?"

"Lots of people. Too many. Security."

"Because of the...Who did you see a few minutes ago?"

"I don't know. A young guy, uh...He was...yeah, young. I only saw him for a few seconds. And then someone was chasing him. A white guy."

Nozipho shook her head. "We'll just wait."

"Until there are fewer of them out there."

"Do you have a better idea?"

"No," Thembinkosi said. "No!" He sniffed loudly. "Did you put on her perfume?"

"Only a little! Really, it was just a dab."

34 Lots of greenery in the fridge. Lettuce, cucumbers, apples, herbs. Other fruits as well. No meat. Several kinds of juice. *A white woman*, Moses thought. *Typical.* He reached for a carton of papaya juice and drank out of it. He knelt down beside the cabinets and turned the spigot on the water canister. Let it run and gulped down water. So incredibly thirsty.

In the bathroom, he pulled a towel off a bar and wiped the sweat from his face and arms. The towel smelled of expensive soap. Moses pressed it against his face and inhaled. He wondered what parts of herself the occupant of this house had dried with this towel. He hung it back up. Would she catch his scent later, too?

Though small, the lounge had been decorated with at least a little good taste. Colorful, no excessive frills. A few photos were sitting in a small cupboard next to the TV. A brunette woman with medium-length hair. A photo with her mama, one with a friend, one with another friend, and yet another with a different friend, who looked Asian. No man in any of them. Maybe she was lesbian. Would make sense. Many lesbians were vegetarian. He'd read that somewhere. Or someone had told him that. Way at the back, there was another photo showing her sitting on the beach wearing a bikini. Next to her, another woman in t-shirt and shorts, perhaps ten years older than her. Moses studied the woman in the bikini who had to be the one living here. Tried to mentally undress her, to imagine her naked. He shook his head. He had other worries. Real worries.

Back in the bathroom, he lifted the toilet lid and peed. As he was about to flush the commode, some impulse made him hesitate. It was best to not be too loud. Someone might be standing at the door, someone who knew that the woman wasn't at home right now. In that case, the sound of flushing would raise red flags.

What should he do now? In here, he was at least safe for the time being. But that safety was only relative to what was going on outside. Who might be searching for him close by? And who might come in the house? And the million-dollar question still hadn't changed: How could he get out of here?

Moses quietly cursed the fact that he was now farther from the exit than he had been a few minutes ago. If he'd been lucky, he might already be looking at the gate. What now? He was about the same distance away as he had been the moment he started running from the two whites. How much time had passed since then? He looked at his watch. It was already two o'clock.

Only two. It had been less than an hour since he'd started trying to escape. And yet, it felt like an eternity to him. And it was still so damned hot. He was dripping in sweat again.

Somewhere, he heard the rising sound of a siren. They were coming with sirens blaring. Moses listened more closely. And then even more closely. There was something about this tone that bothered him.

It slowly dawned on him that what he was hearing wasn't a siren.

 35 The highest ranking of the security personnel sent the two colleagues who had come with him off on foot. As he talked, he gestured vaguely in various directions. Do this, do that. The young man and woman, the rookies, disappeared.

He then turned to the bakkie crew. More pointing and talking. The four guards got back in the bakkie and drove off.

"Should we go now?" Nozipho asked, just as another bakkie pulled up. Central Alert, again. Four people, again. Three of them young: two women, one man. In uniform.

As well as an older white man. At least fifty. A little heavier. It was hard for him to climb down from the driver's seat to the street. Once he emerged, the power structure changed in front of the house. The man who had previously been in charge respectfully approached the white man. Nodded before even a word was spoken.

The chief looked around. *Well?* He asked the question without speaking.

The other man spoke for him. Pointed, gestured, boot-licked. The white man nodded. Reached into his breast pocket and pulled out a phone.

"That doesn't look good," Nozipho said.

"Uh-uh!"

"All because of the boy?"

"Don't know."

"He's calling the cops."

"So what."

"But..."

"What?"

"Nothing!"

"Come on!"

"We'd already agreed that they wouldn't stay here forever."

"They've been here longer than I thought they'd be."

"No... I mean..."

"The two guys in the car? From earlier?"

"Uh-huh."

"But they won't come back in here if the gated community is full of security folks. Not if they're the ones who stuck that woman in the freezer."

"You have a point."

 36 Moses slowly moved away from the terrace door and further into the house.

As he walked by, he glanced once more at the photos, at the picture of the woman in the bikini that stood in the back.

He now knew exactly what he had heard. The kitchen door was there, the bathroom across the hall. Further on was another door, had to be one of the bedrooms. However, Moses strode straight toward the staircase.

He could once again hear the siren that wasn't a siren. He was glad his shoes had soft soles and that the stairs were covered in carpet squares. Eight, nine, ten. Four steps to go. Right before he reached the top, he leaned a little forward. Another hallway, a wardrobe, and two dressers which looked antique. At the end of the hall, a mirror was hanging on the wall at about his height. In the mirror, he caught sight of a bright glow from one of the rooms. The edge of a bed covered in white sheets. Sunlight reflected off the white walls. He was almost blinded.

The sound resumed. Moses moved a step forward. Climbed the final step to the top. Slid his foot further into the hallway. Pulled his body up after it. Very slowly. Then the other foot, followed again by his body.

He could now see the woman's hair in the mirror. Her head

was moving up and down, though simultaneously forward and backward as well. Even without the sound—which was rising and falling, like the body he could partially see—he would have known what was happening. Just a bit farther. He could now see the contours of the brunette's body. Her back, her ass, her breast in profile. Her groaning grew more intense. Just a little farther.

Moses was so far down the hall that he was about to lose sight of the reflection in the mirror. One step to the side, and he had a direct line of vision into the room. Wow. The woman was straddling a man. She wasn't a lesbian at all. The man's legs were stretched underneath the sheet, his body was completely covered by the woman. He could now hear a sound coming from his mouth as well. He was responding with a slow rhythm to the woman's continuous tone. A bass line.

Moses then realized why the space was so bright. Numerous mirrors in all shapes and sizes were hung on the walls, reflecting back the light of day.

He focused again on the woman. She was lifting and thrusting her crotch faster and faster, and Moses could hardly believe his eyes. She was sitting on a black cock. He still couldn't see any other part of the man.

She had to be a foreigner. White South African women never slept with black men. Black men all had AIDS anyway. At least, that's what white women seemed to think.

Hmmm, Moses thought, *they knew each other pretty well.* They weren't using a condom. He felt himself get hard. No wonder. He'd been so excited at the thought of having sex with Sandi. And he was now watching two other people make love. Of course, he didn't have to, but he couldn't seem to stop. What a beautiful woman. Her movements simply aroused him even though she was straddling another man. Just a little more to the side. He was now standing at the wall on which the large mirror was hanging, the one he had just been staring into. The man was no longer young. He could see part of his head. Bald actually, but the stubble was silvery. He now raised his arms and reached for the woman's buttocks, slowly brushing his fingers across her skin. The woman lifted her head and breathed deeply. As she did this, she opened her eyes. In the mirror on the wall next to the bed, he could see her aroused face. Her hair clung in sweaty tendrils across her eyes and nose.

Moses realized all he needed to have done was glance out of one of the house's front windows, where he would have probably seen two cars, and known instantly that he wasn't alone in the house. Rookie mistake. Well, he wasn't exactly an experienced burglar. He wondered if it was time for him to disappear, regardless of how much he was enjoying what he was watching. One more look, he told himself. The woman's movements were slowing down. She was brushing her hair back with one hand while she gazed forward contentedly.

That was the moment their eyes met. Moses froze there in the hallway. The woman's eyes widened as she went through the endless transformation, the escalating and highly complex process that evolved from seeing and comprehension to classification and confirmation. Her body, which had been so relaxed and lovely, now went rigid. Right before her eyes were about to leave their sockets, she emitted a high-pitched, panicked scream.

Moses spun around and dashed down the stairs.

 "Where are you going?" Nozipho asked.

"To the garage."

"Why?"

"If I have to spend some time with her under one roof, I want to know who she is," Thembinkosi said. "Was," he amended.

"How?"

"We're going to check her out." Thembinkosi opened the door to the garage. Switched on the dim light.

"But she's dead."

"Of course, she's dead." He was already lifting the lid.

"No!"

"Yes!"

"Why?"

"Because we have time. And because we don't know what we might be able to get out of it."

"I'm not touching her. It brings bad luck."

"To whom?"

"Don't make fun of me."

Thembinkosi was still holding the freezer lid. "Hold it up!"

Nozipho shook her head.

Thembinkosi shut the chest again. Looked around. Walked straight across the garage. A broom was standing close to the outer garage door. He returned with the broom. Opened the chest again and propped the lid up with the broom handle.

"Did you straighten everything up in the bedroom?" he asked, bending over the freezer.

"Yes. Looks like it did before. What did you think I did? I stuck the empty hangers under the underwear in one of the drawers."

Thembinkosi thought about the shirts he had stuffed into his briefcase. He'd left the hangers on the rod.

He ran his hands over the body. Pockets. Change. He felt inside the t-shirt pocket. Thought about rigor mortis, which he'd heard about on some crime show. Pulled out a piece of plastic.

"Well?" Nozipho asked.

He looked at the plastic card. Health Care. A name.

"Celeste Rubin." A number, too. "Maybe she was at the doctor's this morning."

"So what....What are you doing?"

Thembinkosi was halfway in the chest, attempting to flip over the body. He had stuck his hands under the corpse and was tugging at her jeans. However, the body wasn't cooperating.

"Help me!"

"No," Nozipho said. "How?" she then asked.

Thembinkosi propped his arms on the edge of the chest. "Let's pull her out."

"What? Why would we do that?"

"I want to know what else she has on her." He leaned back into the freezer and grabbed the corpse's feet with both hands. "Help me!" The feet were already up on the edge of the freezer. "Come on!"

Nozipho reached into the arctic climate and wrapped both hands around one of her arms. She was pulling with all her strength when the fabric of her dress ripped. She immediately dropped the arm.

"Shit!" she cried. "Look what happened!"

It was only a tiny tear. Thembinkosi had a hard time not laughing while keeping his grip on the feet.

"Just look at that!" Nozipho grumbled. "It's ruined."

The tear was at the tightest spot. Nozipho's slip now peeked through, but if she carried her purse just right, no one would notice it.

"Only whites run around like this," she said, turning away slightly.

Thembinkosi could tell she was close to tears. Nozipho was always cool, methodical. Together they had robbed from both the rich and the not-so-rich for four years now. She was always up to the challenge and had always stayed composed.

"Wait!" he said, while at the same moment he managed to pull the body the rest of the way out of the chest. Only the shoulders were still resting on the edge. One last effort, a pull, and her head hit the garage floor. It sounded like a piece of china with a crack in it.

Nozipho screamed and now started to sob.

Thembinkosi dropped the corpse's legs and took his wife into his arms. "Strange day!" he said.

"Shitty day!" she shot back. "I don't want to do these crappy role-playing games anymore. I want to break in like I learned it from you. Grab the stuff and disappear. Secretly, as it's supposed to be."

"Uh-huh. Maybe we need to change our strategy a little."

They kissed, and then looked back in the freezer. Spinach. Pizza. Shrimp in clear plastic boxes. Meat of all kinds. They glanced at each other. Nozipho was the first one to start laughing. "Corpse on a bed of spinach!" she said, drying her tears.

"White people are cannibals!" Thembinkosi added, snorting with laughter.

They hugged each other again. Kissed.

"I love you," Thembinkosi said.

"I love you, too," Nozipho said.

They stayed with their arms around each other for a few more seconds. "We have to get out of here!" Nozipho insisted.

"You're right! But I still want to see what she has on her."

Thembinkosi bent down, and for the first time, he examined the body closely. Facial bruising. She'd been hit. Or did that come from the deep freezing? A wound in her hair. She hadn't been all that old. It was hard to tell when it came to age. However, Ma Jordan, who lived next door to his sister, was 65, and she was clearly older than the woman lying at his feet. She would never get to be 65. Her hair was gray, her face somehow...He thought she looked surprised, but chose not to say anything about it. The bright t-shirt and denim shorts screamed free time, her feet were bare. Thembinkosi flipped over the body. Reached into her back pocket and pulled out an ID.

"Celeste Rubin," he said again. "She's 57." The photo was a few years old. Thembinkosi felt around the other pocket. Empty. "Let's put her back in."

"I can't," Nozipho declared. "The dress won't make it."

"True."

He turned Celeste onto her back, then he reached under her armpits and slowly straightened up. *A person like this is heavy*, he thought. And this person was really cold, too. Much colder than she had been just a few minutes ago. He lifted the body over the edge of the freezer and released it.

The containers of frozen food clattered.

Thembinkosi shut the chest. "Or would you like to take the shrimp with us? You love them."

"But not frozen ones. Idiot!" Nozipho reminded him. She was holding the door open that led from the garage to the house.

38 Moses jumped down the last few steps to the lounge. He lost his footing on a runner that lay in his path. He quickly scrambled to his feet as he heard footsteps on the floor above. Also the couple's voices, but he couldn't understand anything they were saying. All he had to do was push open the terrace door. Out and back in the direction from which he'd come. Just had to make sure to not get any further away from the exit.

Rapidly cleared the hedges and walls. The other guy wouldn't run after him. Moses had seen the condition he'd been in. Around the corner in the outer wall and right on going. Another jump, solid landing, keep running. All of a sudden, the man in the rugby shirt was standing in front of him. He wasn't fit or all that fast, at least he didn't look like it. But he was standing in his way. Moses knocked him down. And got caught. The sharks guy was clinging to him. He had wrapped his arms around both of Moses' legs.

"We know what you did!" he cried.

Moses tried to kick free, but in vain. The other man had strong arms.

"You won't get out of here!" the rugby man said as his breath grew shorter.

But the kicking still wasn't helping. Moses swung at the man's head. First with his hand, then with his fist. The man clutched at his head with one hand, trying to protect it. As he did that, he tightened his grip with the other hand. Moses was still lying half on top of him. Kick harder, break his grip. He was slowly gaining more maneuvering room. Moses only needed a second. He stretched out his right leg and then brought his knee up hard. It landed in the middle of the rugby man's face.

He hollered in pain.

Then, there was another voice.

"Help!" a woman screamed. "He's killing him! Helllllp!"

Moses had already freed himself by the time the woman who had come out of the house nailed him with a plastic chair in his lower back. *Keep running*, he told himself.

But instead he stayed where he was and tried to deflect the next blow. Pulling back his arm, he slapped the woman hard across the face. As his body twisted with the momentum, he heard more than saw her glasses land somewhere. By the time Moses tightened his muscles for the next jump, the woman had begun to cry.

 "They're still standing there," Thembinkosi said.

"More keep coming," Nozipho added. "They're going to a lot of trouble. How many do you think there are?"

"By this point? I've seen about fifteen of them. Maybe more."

"And then there's the ones you probably haven't seen. Shit."

"But why are they standing around here of all places?"

"I was wondering that, too," Nozipho agreed. Outside, the older white man had gathered several uniformed guards around him. He was giving orders. "I think this has to be the central street through the gated community."

"I'd stay up at the exit."

"Another group is probably already set up there."

"And you think the rest of them are staying around here because this is the main street."

"Can you think of any other reason?"

"Shit," Thembinkosi said. "Then it's a good thing we did that with the clothes."

"What should we do? Head straight for the exit?"

"Straight for the exit."

"Now?"

"Uh-huh."

"And if something goes wrong?"

"What could go wrong?"

Nozipho had to think about this for a second. "Well... If the security people know this area, they might know that we don't live here."

"So? We could be visiting."

"But what if they know that these people..." Nozipho hesitated. "Look around. They don't have any black friends!"

"Fine. Then we're business partners."

"And what kind of business are these people in?"

Thembinkosi considered this for a moment. "We might be buying a car from them."

"Okay," Nozipho concurred. "We could be doing that. It might work."

"Regardless, we won't have to justify anything. We're simply two people who have walked out of this house and want to go somewhere else. For example, to the exit."

"But if we just bought a car from them...Why are we walking?"

40 Gerrit van Lange stood on the street that ran through the center of the gated community and thought about the fact he was slowly getting too old for situations like this. Not because he couldn't get the upper hand anymore. He was an old hat at this, experienced in the struggles for physical safety and undamaged property. He had been through more than enough of these stories. But what could he do? He was still a few years away from retirement. And he had no training to do anything except the job he currently had. Security. When you managed a security company, you couldn't simply retrain for something else.

His phone rang.

"What's going on?"

Van Lange listened, interjecting an occasional "Yes!" He

rolled his eyes at the people gathered around and watching him. He then exhaled through his lips and added one more "Yes!" When the conversation eventually came to an end, he added an "Uiuiuiuiui!"

He walked over to his car and picked up the radio receiver. Pressed the button: "Listen everyone. Our suspect is back on the run. He's about twenty years old. In jeans and a yellow t-shirt. A conspicuous afro." Van Lange paused. After this incident, he would need to instruct his people to knuckle down a little harder for a few weeks. Until he started to get calls from people complaining about rough treatment. Or about friends or relatives who had been harassed or asked to show their IDs. To hell with that! "We have no idea," he continued, "how long he's been in here, but we do know the following: He broke in a house and stole jewelry and cash. A pretty good haul. He then tried to rape a woman." Van Lange took a moment to consider his next comment, but why should he hide it? "A white woman," he added. "And then he brutally assaulted an older couple."

He ended the radio connection. He should actually call the police. There was enough justification to do that. But from past experience, he knew his people's attentiveness would wane as soon as they knew the cops were on their way. And besides, where the cops were concerned, you never really knew if they would show up.

He pressed the radio button again: "We will do everything to locate this criminal and bring him down. And...if you must use force...do it in God's name."

 Moses felt pain in his back. The woman had hit him as hard as she could. He hadn't done anything to either one of them. Maybe they knew the white woman in whose house he'd just been. Had she called them? Nonsense. Had they heard the screams? The distance was too far. He now had to get away from the outer wall, because there was only one way out of here. One which led away from the wall. One more leap, and he would return to the street to run. That was easier and would go faster.

A low hedge, stop, take the curve to the right, and slip between a house and a medium-height wall.

A female guard was walking toward him from the other side of the street. Shit. He came to an abrupt stop and ran back. The woman called out something. He took the next cut-through. Bad call. A sturdily built man stood there, grinning at him. He should have risked it with the woman. Although...You couldn't be sure about anything these days. What he couldn't do was stay put. He kept running and jumped at the man. Outstretched leg in the stomach. The guy collapsed and stayed on the ground. Moses kept running. Finally on the street. Turned left and continued running. Just don't stop. A quick glance back. There were people. Not close.

Run.

He was sweating buckets.

Were these security guards carrying guns? *Run*, Moses thought. *Just run.*

 "Should we?" Nozipho asked.

She tugged the dress straight and pivoted in front of Thembinkosi. Purse on her shoulder. She took a sniff under her arm. Wrinkled her nose.

"Yes...although...wait..."

"What is it?

"Just wait," he said again. And then: "Come on!"

"What?"

"Just come!"

Nozipho walked over to the window. A third car was now sitting outside, covered by a section of the wall along the street. An old station wagon. A door opened, and a man stepped out. "Shit!" she said. "What should we do now?"

"Is that them? Have they come back?"

"How should I know?

"You're the one who saw them," Thembinkosi said.

"No, I didn't."

Two men in casual clothes were standing beside the white man. The one had curly hair, the other was bald. Both in jeans. The officer was telling them something, gesturing. The men nodded. One of them pointed at the house in which they were hiding. We can go in there, right?

The bald guy looked at his companion and pointed at the garage.

Thembinkosi grabbed Nozipho's hand and picked up the briefcase. He pulled her into the smaller of the two bedrooms. Opened one of the doors to the wardrobe he'd looked in so long ago. Pushed her inside, closing the door behind her. Then vanished behind the adjacent door.

Both of them heard the squeaking of an unoiled garage door. Up. Engine noise. Then down.

 Insane, Moses thought as he dashed down the street. First, the referee and the other white guy. And now the security people. Their numbers were increasing. And yet, all he had was an old car that wouldn't start, which was why he needed help. But he had already assaulted three people. And interrupted two others having sex. Which was more serious?

And what would've happened if he'd just let the referee...

Screeching tires. Up ahead, yet another silver-and-blue vehicle. A bakkie that was speeding toward him. Moses glanced around. He was back in bungalow land. One-storied houses. Closer to the exit. Good.

But the car was driving at him. Very bad.

He decided to stay where he was standing for a moment. The car raced toward him. A small property wall to his right, less than a meter tall, and behind it a nicely manicured lawn. To his left, tall weeds and car parts in front of the front door. No hiding places on either side.

The bakkie didn't slow down. On the contrary.

The bakkie was still forty meters away. Moses tensed his muscles. Twenty meters. Still wasn't braking.

The bakkie had almost reached him. Three.

Two. One.

Moses threw himself to the right and rolled to the side. The driver hit his brakes hard.

Moses' shoulder slammed into something. He leaped to his feet. Dashed across the perfect lawn. Saw some kind of movement inside the house, didn't have time to concentrate on it. Heard the bakkie slam into reverse. Between several terraces and back doors. Finally stopped for a moment. Breathe evenly. His heart beat in unison.

"He's back here!" A woman's voice. Behind him. In the house with the super-lawn? No time to look back.

In front of him, a row of bungalows. Beyond it, another street.

Crap. The referee was also in front of him. Had just caught sight of a patch of blue from his t-shirt.

The referee had also seen him. Was walking toward him. Wait a second longer. Lure him over. Away from the street. Then back again.

Moses took the next cut-through. The bungalow was now to his right. A wall that increased in height, step by step, to his left. If he had given the referee enough time, he wouldn't turn around but would run after him.

This was the next street. A little further to his left was a nanny with a small white child. Moses couldn't tell if it was a boy or a girl.

The nanny shook her head. Not in her direction? Is that what she meant? The other direction seemed empty.

From where the nanny and child were standing came another voice. "Is he out there?"

Moses crossed the street. Dove headfirst over a knee-high wall and landed on a bag of trash. He remained stretched out on the ground and waited for something to happen.

44 The garage door rolled down.

"Didn't I tell you?" A high masculine voice. No answer to the question.

"You almost lost it." The same voice. Pissing in the toilet. Followed by flushing.

"You know what?" Again the high voice. "It's funny how long you can smell perfume. I mean...Gwen's been gone... How long is her training? Five days. And yet that perfume is still in the air. I can smell it so clearly. Really weird."

The sound of boots in the house. "I gave her that for her birthday, remember? The salesgirl had just looked at me when I'd asked her about it. Well...you know already. And then I gave her a super sexy slip as well. Hot. Really hot. You know."

Thembinkosi grew warm. Hopefully, High Voice wouldn't want to show the other man the slip. Was that what he had? In his jacket pocket? And had Nozipho really tidied up the bedroom?

"What should we do now?" Again, High Voice.

"Can you shut up for just a second?" Notably deeper, different. Someone who didn't say much.

"Of course!" High Voice. "You know I can keep my trap shut. But that was awesome with the security guys out there. I mean..."

"Just be quiet!"

"Okay. Okay."

Footsteps. The boots and other shoes. Was High Voice wearing soft soles? Quiet squeaking on the floor. What kind of floor was that anyway? Didn't matter. *Tiles*, Thembinkosi thought, *of course.* It was hotter in the wardrobe than it was outside of it. He wanted to wipe the sweat from his face, but it was too tight for that.

He very cautiously scratched the wardrobe partition that separated him from Nozipho. A responding scratch came instantly from the other side.

"What should we do now?" High Voice. "We can't just

take her out of here now."

"No, we can't!"

45 Moses cowered behind the wall. Half on the trash bag, half off. A dead bird was lying next to his head. Dark with a streak of red. Ants had already begun blazing a trail to start the evisceration process. *Just lie here for a bit,* he thought. Had the nanny warned him? Black solidarity?

Maybe that's what it was. A few black families had to be living in here. Somewhere he was bound to be able to get help. He recalled the Kaizer Chiefs banner in the window. That had been ages ago. He looked at his watch. 2:06.

"Is he over here?" Moses heard a voice. That was the white guy with the club.

"No, boss!" The nanny.

"If you see him… let me know!"

"Yes, boss!" She was actually helping him. Good woman. A motor. Brakes.

"He isn't here." The white guy. On the street right in front of him.

"He tried to rape a woman!" What?

A black voice. Masculine. "Hurt a whole bunch of people. He's dangerous! And broke into an old man's house."

Moses listened as the white man struck his hand with his club. "I'm ready for him!" The car drove off.

Were they really talking about me? Moses wondered.

Nothing happened for a few seconds. Then a shadow over him. The white guy was sitting on the wall, his ass directly above him. Not even ten centimeters away.

Moses heard the click of a lighter. The white man was smoking. He also wanted to smoke.

"Oh," said the nanny in a strangely artificial tone. "The ball's gone now." Short pause. "Who's going to get the ball for us?"

The shadow above him evaporated. A ball was kicked.

"Look," she said. "Isn't that a nice man?"

What a smart woman, Moses thought, taking a deep breath.

46 Thud. That was the door to the garage again. No steps or voices could be heard.

Thembinkosi opened the wardrobe door and breathed more freely.

He tugged open the other door and gazed into Nozipho's eyes.

"I want out of here," she said.

"Me, too. But we can't now."

"But how long will we have to wait?"

"Until it's safe."

"Maybe we should consider a career change."

"Maybe. If they can't get rid of the body right now, they might leave again."

"Too many maybes!"

"Possibly."

"Sorry about the perfume. That was too risky."

"It turned out okay."

"Uh-huh, just barely," Nozipho said. "We're doubly stuck now. Because of the security people, and now because of the two guys in the house."

"We just need a little patience, okay? They'll disappear soon."

The door to the garage opened again.

"Are you sure," asked Deep Voice, "she had her ID on her?"

Thembinkosi rolled his eyes. Pointed at his pants pocket. That was where Celeste Rubin's ID was. He climbed back into the wardrobe.

"Yes." High Voice. "Where's her suitcase?"

"I need to pee," he heard Nozipho whisper.

Then, there were footsteps in the room.

47 Willie hit his club into his left hand. He knew he did that too often. A habit that had already caused a thin callus to build up. However, whenever he stood spread-legged in front of a young black man, he made an impression doing it. That much was obvious.

The rich have it good, he thought, as he sat down on the little wall. These large houses with their neat lawns. Compared to his tiny place in Stoney Drift...it wasn't fair. It had been years since he'd had enough left over to stick into the house. Then again, who in that shabby neighborhood did? Except for a few coloreds who'd been moving into the settlement in increasing numbers in recent years.

I've had to cut corners on cigarettes, too, Willie thought as he lit a Chesterfield.

The nanny was playing ball with the little boy. Looked ridiculous. She walked up to the ball and kicked it hard. Much too far for the little boy. The rich did indeed have it good. Someone was always there for their kids. Although... He never would have trusted his children to a black woman. They were all with Janice now anyway, the cow.

"Oh! The ball's gone now," the dumb nanny said. "Who's going to get the ball for us?" she asked annoyingly.

Considering how fat she was, it would probably take years if she did it herself. The little boy stared into the sky. Willie inhaled deeply one more time before getting to his feet. It was time to find that bastard anyway. He held the smoke in his lungs until he reached the ball and then ex-haled it slowly. He very carefully kicked the ball to the boy who was laughing at him.

"Look!" the nanny said as she raised her hands. "What a nice man!"

The guy was nowhere in sight. Willie turned around a couple of times before walking up the street. They would catch him, of course. He wouldn't get away from here all that easily.

A couple of Central Alert people were waiting for him at

the exit. And there was no way he was going to make it over the wall.

 Somebody was walking through the room. Thembinkosi heard a zipper being opened. The sound of rummaging. Re-packing.

"Well?" Deep Voice had to be standing at the door.

"Nothing." High Voice.

"When did you see the ID?"

"When you hit her in the face. Well...not the first time. Later on sometime. When she fell down out in the hallway. When you kicked her in the side and spat on her. That was when I saw the ID in her jeans pocket. The back one. It was sticking out a little."

"And then what happened?"

"Then you turned her over and hit her some more."

Neither of them said anything for a few seconds, then High Voice continued.

"Because she didn't want to talk."

Another pause. High Voice again. "I didn't see the ID after that."

"So, it's either still on her body, or it fell out of her pocket." Deep Voice. "Let's check her out one more time. I don't want that thing to get found. Either here in the house or where we're going to dump her."

Footsteps. Door slamming. Garage door, too. Thembinkosi opened his door the same moment Nozipho did hers.

 The white man's boots could be heard for a few seconds. Moses then crawled slowly around the house. He had briefly considered thanking the nanny. With a wave. A nod. But he didn't want to put her in any danger. She understood as it was. Behind the house, he crept along another wall whose height decreased in steps down to the hedge. He was peeking through the hedge into the next yard when it occurred to him that he hadn't had the time to verify that he wasn't being watched from the house he'd just crawled by.

Moses raised his head and realized this wasn't enough for him to get a good sightline. He moved back a short way and sat up with his back against the wall. Breathed slower. Deeper. And sensed how tired he actually was. And how hungry. Coffee and bread for breakfast, that was it. And the moving for Prof. Brinsley. And then here.

No idea where he was inside The Pines. The last escape from the referee, the guards, the security vehicle, and the white guy...*Shit,* he thought. Whoever had been sitting in the security car...That had been an attempt to kill him.

Why?

He needed a few moments to remember. Rape. That word had tumbled out when someone in that vehicle had chatted with the white guy. Was that the same car that had tried to run him down?

And the rape? Someone else had to be on foot in here. They couldn't mean him.

The movement at the upper edge of his vision was barely noticeable. Moses looked up and met the curious eyes of a little girl. She was three or four years old with blonde braids dangling on each side of her face. In the glow of the sunshine from where she was standing behind the window, she looked like a character in a children's book. She waved at him. He waved back.

If she caught sight of a black man creeping around her yard, she wasn't thinking, "Mommy, a black man is crawling around our yard." But what was she thinking? He had to get out of here. Wherever a small child happened to be, an adult wasn't far behind. And they would definitely ask, "Why the hell is a black man crawling around our yard?"

If only he could figure out where he was. And where was Sandi?

50 "Are we on the air? Skype is amazing. Hello? Ah... now! All right...I'll start since I know the two of you. Inspector Pokwana in Beacon Bay and Warren Kramer in... Ah yes, you're both in Beacon Bay. Neighbors, practically. So Inspector Pokwana is the police contact officer for the Neighborhood Community Watch in Dorchester Heights. Hello..."

"Hello!"

"And Warren is responsible for the security of the gated communities managed by Meyer Investment. Hi, Warren."

"Stevie, hi."

"That's six of them, right, Warren? Gated Communities. Man, it's warm today..."

"Exactly. Six. Yes, here in the office it's unbearable."

"Okay. So we all know what's happened. A dangerous individual is on the loose in The Pines. A young man. Broke in and stole numerous items of value. Tried to rape a, uh, woman. Hurt one of our colleagues, who's now on his way to the hospital with bruised balls, as I've been told. Dad is on site and has everything under control. But we still don't have the guy."

"I've sent around the photo taken from the cctv footage. Did you get it?"

"Hm!" Warren.

"Yes." Pokwana.

"Recognize him?"

"Never seen him," Pokwana said.

"Me, neither." Stevie van Lange paused. "We have a ton of people in The Pines, and I think we'll catch him soon. However, in my opinion... if he puts up a fight, it could get quite dicey. And we don't know if he's armed. So we thought—Dad's idea—that we could maybe temporarily shut down the access roads."

"Absolutely not," Pokwana interjected. "The neighborhood's too large. How would you manage that? Too many people live there."

"I was thinking we could help each other out. People will soon be coming home from work."

"We'll send a third car over. We really can't swing more than that. And if he really is all that dangerous, then my people will be needed inside the neighborhood, not at the gate. Besides, that'll be hard enough as it is. We can't stop people who live half a kilometer away from where we're searching for the suspect from getting home."

"Do we know where he is?" van Lange asked.

"Can't you just suggest it to people?" Kramer.

"Suggest what?" Pokwana.

"That they wait outside until we have him."

"Uh-huh. We could." Pokwana. "We could try."

"So we'll post a few people at the entrance and...what?" That was van Lange. "It's best to stay outside, otherwise... I think I'll just drive over there myself. What time is it? Ten past two. I can get there in fifteen minutes. Warren, what about you?"

"I'll join you."

"And you, Inspector Pokwana?"

"Let me first talk to my people. I mean...a single fellow. That can't be all that hard."

51 "What did they do to her?" Nozipho shook her head.

"Yeah. And above all, why?"

"They beat and kicked her. Imagine that. And they spit on her, too."

"Uh-huh. Main thing, they killed her."

"Pigs."

"Hmm...We could try to get out of here."

"But if we open this door and they come back from the garage at that moment, we're dead."

"True. We'll also get beaten and kicked, as well as spat on."

"What should we do? I still need to pee."

"I don't know."

"We could call for help. Out the window."

"But the security guys just saw the whites walk into this house. If we call for help, they'll shoot at us."

"You're exaggerating."

"Maybe."

"What a shitty situation."

"It's totally a shitty situation."

The door to the garage opened. Thembinkosi and Nozipho vanished back into the wardrobe.

 Moses broke through the hedge with his shoulder. His t-shirt ripped down the side as he did that. He crawled on all fours into the shadow of the next house. No time to look around. Another street was located on the other side of the house. They would be patrolling everywhere by now. He couldn't stay outside much longer. He couldn't stay anywhere much longer. Around the house. *How many houses have I already had to creep around*, he wondered.

On his stomach to the next wall. Almost shoulder high. He slowly straightened up to look over it. First forward, then toward the back. Risk assessment. Crown of his head, forehead, eyes. Houses on the other side of the street, as usual. A security car rolled by. Nothing unusual.

Look around. Curtains shut. An empty house. Presumably.

Another security vehicle on the other side of the wall. Or the same one. Yet another Polo. He'd seen Polos—had to be more than one—and the bakkie that had tried to hit him. Another car drove by, then another. Moses scanned for signs of life in the houses across the way. Didn't see any. The workday hadn't ended yet. People were still at the office. And nobody was watching him from there.

Had he already been along here? The streets all looked the same. One-storied houses across the street, and if he turned right, he could see the ones with two stories. What would have happened if he had just surrendered to the two whites? Right at the beginning...

They would have called the police and beaten him.

No. They would have beaten him and then called the police. He had fought back. *We didn't have a choice*, they'd have said.

In the station, the cops would have beaten him some more. One of them might have even raped him. Or a cellmate would have taken care of that. Or several of them. And the cops would have stood there and watched.

They would have left him lying there until morning and then set him free with a kick in the ass.

He'd been right to run.

 Mrs. Viljoen went to her telephone. The older she grew, the longer it took her to cover the distance to the dresser in the hallway. She really needed to get people to start calling her on her cell phone. But that was expensive.

"Yes?"

"Did you hear?" Rose was extremely excited.

"What?"

"George was robbed."

"What?"

"In broad daylight!"

"Really?"

"Everything's gone!"

"Everything?"

"A black!"

"Hng!"

"A young black man! And everything's gone. The jewelry. You know how attached he was to those things. All those mementos from Margaret. He's in an awful state. Just think. You haven't seen anything? Not even the security people? There's so many of them. All you need to do is look out your window. They say they're going to catch him. He was even in my garden. Just think. He might have broken in my place, too. They don't respect any boundaries. My sister always says it was wrong to get rid of the death penalty. Just think.

At least he wouldn't do it again. And a woman's been raped. I don't know her. She's new here. What do you think?"

Mrs. Viljoen didn't say anything. You didn't wish things like this on anyone, but, well, they happened anyway. Even in a safe neighborhood like The Pines.

"My dear, I can tell you're at a loss for words over all this," Rose continued. "And what's been going on with you?"

 Nozipho listened through the wardrobe door. The room door had been shut from the hallway. She was trying to hear what the two whites were saying. She recognized the voices. That wasn't difficult. But she couldn't make out all the words.

"...car...," she understood. High Voice.

And again: "...car...," this time Deep Voice.

The same word again and then once more, then several words from High Voice, "...we couldn't have guessed... what's actually going on here?...other plan..."

The other man said something, but for a long time, all she could hear was the voice and not the words it was saying. Then the voice grew clearer. Perhaps he had turned around. "I won't haul her off in an open vehicle."

Footsteps. The garage door slammed shut. Squeaking. A motor turning over, then the sound of the garage door again.

"What are they doing?" she heard Thembinkosi say.

"Something with a car."

"They're going to dump the body."

"Not yet. Not with that car. People can see in it."

"What now?" Thembinkosi asked.

"How would I know? In any case, one of them has left. To get another car."

 How could someone get out of a gated community? Through the gate you entered through. But how could he get back to the gate?

Moses was still standing behind the shoulder-high wall, trying to figure out where he was. The walls, the electrified wire, and the surveillance conveyed the message that nobody was allowed in unless they belonged here. All the burglars and tramps, all the poor and disadvantaged, you needed to defend yourself against. It was the same regardless of where you had to live in South Africa. But he wanted to get out. He hadn't come here voluntarily.

But how to get out? And where? Was there something like an emergency exit here? A gated community didn't need a fire escape or an evacuation plan. After all, there was only the one exit. He had to get there. But how? The security company's bakkie drove across his field of vision. An older black man was sitting at the wheel. A few minutes ago, he hadn't even paid attention to who was driving the car that tried to run him down.

Maybe the nanny could help him. He should have asked her. The first friendly person he'd encountered in here. Moses ducked and crept back to the parallel street. He heard the white guy's voice again.

"If I were in charge here, none of this would have gotten so far."

"What do you mean?" a second voice asked. Also masculine. Also white. Also no longer young. Was that the referee? He couldn't remember how his voice sounded.

"You know what I mean."

"Yes…" The second voice sounded teacherly. "It's different than it used to be. Be careful. You don't want to end up in trouble when all's said and done."

"Burglary. Rape. Who knows what else he's up to?"

The two men were standing on the other side of the wall. Moses tried not to breathe.

"Still, there shouldn't be any shooting unless it's an emergency. Got it?"

"Yeah, yeah…Sure, only in an emergency."

"And even then…Think about what the newspapers will write about it."

The footsteps faded. Moses began to breathe again.

 56   "Which of the two of them has left?" Thembinkosi leaned out of the wardrobe. His door opened in such a way that he couldn't see out the window.

"No idea," Nozipho said. "I only saw the car driving away."

The garage door slammed. A phone rang.

"Yes," High Voice said.

Thembinkosi stepped back into the wardrobe and nodded at Nozipho. They both left the doors behind which they were hiding open a crack. Air circulation.

"Everything's fine," High Voice said. "No, Mother's doing well." He had to be standing right outside the room. "Yes, she went shopping. Uh-huh... I'll tell her. She probably has her phone turned off again. Sure. Yes, I love you, too. Take care."

A few moments later, High Voice was in the kitchen. He opened a cupboard and pulled out a glass.

"His mother?" Nozipho asked quietly.

"His mother-in-law."

"Are you sure?"

"No, just a feeling."

The sound of a bottle being opened in the kitchen. Something was poured into a glass. Drawers.

"What should we do?"

"Either we wait. Or we do something." Thembinkosi exhaled through his lips.

"What could we do?"

Thembinkosi stepped out of the wardrobe. Spoke quietly. "As soon as we leave this room, we'll face a confrontation. We'll have to..."

"...incapacitate him. They murdered that woman. We can't tell him that we just happened to be in this house and now want to leave, and that we promise not to say anything."

The shrill siren of a police car in the distance.

"Great," Nozipho said. "And now the cops. They were feeling left out."

57 Moses was still sitting with his back against the wall. He could breathe again, but his legs didn't want to obey. The white trash guy was dreaming of blowing him away. That meant he had a gun on him that would enable him to do that. Every street he crossed from this point on might be his last one. The guy could be standing anywhere, waiting to just shoot him. *I felt threatened*, he would say afterward. Scared of a burglar and rapist. After his death, nobody would give a shit what the newspapers printed.

He didn't want to die.

He needed to be more careful.

Back on all fours. That alone was humiliating. And back in the other direction. The first house. Then the next. The girl's face was no longer in sight. Cautiously. There were probably people at home. They probably knew what was going on in the neighborhood and were now more diligent than usual.

Moses peered around the corner of the house at the street on which the nanny had just been playing ball with the little boy. He couldn't see them anywhere. Or hear them. So keep going. Running the few meters to the wall behind which he had hidden several minutes ago, he threw himself back down in the grass. The dead bird was still being disemboweled by the ants. He lifted his head and looked in both directions, but couldn't see either the nanny or the child.

Lowered, then lifted his head again. For thoroughness' sake. Who else might help him? A guard appeared at the next corner. Moses immediately ducked back down.

Wait. Let him pass. Disappear. Then look for the Kaizer Chiefs' house. The footsteps slowly grew closer. Rubber-soled boots, not loud but audible. Only a few meters away. Moses wished he was as tiny as the ants close to him.

For a long second, Moses heard no noise at all. Each noise seemed to have vanished, to have been swallowed up like under a bell. There were also no smells. And his attempt to feel was just as futile as his attempt to hear. The blood had drained from his fingers and toes. No circulation.

Stasis. Complete. Practically dead.

Tried to quietly breathe in. And back out. In. Back out. Where was the guy?

The blow from the club almost deafened him. It landed on the wall, not on his body, but Moses jerked so hard he almost pissed himself.

"I got him!" the guard yelled, grabbing Moses' feet at the same moment.

It took an eternity for Moses to recover from the shock. Might have been a half or full second. At first, he thrashed about helplessly, then with more determination. He was able to pull up his knees, which destabilized the guard. He then stretched his legs back out. As fast as he could. He hit the guard in his support leg and heard something crack. It was so loud and clear that it seemed like it wanted to make up for the seconds of total silence.

Very close by, he could hear the siren of a police car.

 Sandi was standing in her room. She was convinced at least twenty minutes had passed. Maybe more. The phone was still in her hand. Sweat trickled down her back.

The room was small. Bed and wardrobe and kitchenette in less than twenty square meters. Toilet and shower in an old supply closet. She wasn't complaining. Some of her friends had it even worse. Communal kitchens were shit. Communal bathrooms were shit, in the literal sense. Above all, when the boys used them. She gazed at the small photo of her and Moses that she'd pinned up over her bed.

What had Moses gotten himself into now?

Wrong question. She shook her head. Disloyal. A betrayal to their relationship.

Once more from the top. What had actually happened

to Moses? The car, his phone, the gated community—why would anyone want to live in such a hell hole—the two white men, and then the break-in.

What could I do? she wondered. Nothing came to her. Just like a few minutes ago, and the time before, and the time before that. But there was always something you could do. Right?

So once again. Sandi sat down on the bed and pulled her shoes on. It gave her the feeling of doing something. *Go stand at the entrance to that gated community,* she thought. But how? With whom? With what?

With guns.

Ridiculous. She didn't know anyone who had any. Except for her uncle in Mthatha. Just go in. Search. Take Moses by the arm. Walk out.

Sandi rummaged around under her bed. Pulled out a shoebox. Opened the lid. Pulled out a few maps. Flipped through them. Zimbabwe. Lesotho. Durban.

She left her room and knocked on her neighbor's door. Laura opened right away.

"You have a city map, don't you?" Laura had moved from Zambia three months ago. And had her own car. How else would she find her way around?

"Sure."

"May I borrow it?"

Two minutes later, the map was stretched out on the bed in Sandi's room. She was kneeling beside it. Here was Abbotsford, situated at a highway intersection. Mostly small single-family homes and a few newer gated communities. And there was Dorchester Heights, larger homes, a subdivision stretched along the Nahoon River. Suburbia lifted out of a dictionary, and not even a single shop where you could just buy a loaf of bread. The map didn't show her where The Pines was located. But there couldn't be all that many possibilities. The river was here, Dorchester Heights was there, just as it was printed on the map.

There weren't many other open spaces. She could envision

quite precisely where Moses was. What she couldn't envision was how she was going to actually help him.

59 The security guy instantly released his hold on Moses. From his mouth emerged a sound of surprise, more than of pain.

Stand up, quickly look around. Nobody else was nearby. Back around the house. His ears were still throbbing from the blow that hadn't even struck him. Had he been seen from inside this time? No time to worry about that. Quickly into the next yard. Pause at the wall where he had earlier eavesdropped on the white guy with the club and the other voice. They would shoot him. He had to escape, but he also needed to be careful.

The street was empty. No face in a window, as far as he could see. The two white men had headed to the left. He took off to the right. That was the wrong direction. Away from the exit. Once again. *Then again, if this was about survival*, he thought, *there actually wasn't a wrong direction*.

Moses sprinted down the street and saw the small hill off to his right. So, he was heading toward the river. That was the direction he'd taken at the beginning. A T-intersection in front of him, twenty or thirty meters off. He'd cover the distance rapidly. But which way after he did? Right or left? *Make up your mind*, Moses chided himself.

To the right of the intersection, three people materialized. Moses slowed down slightly.

Two old women and an old man. The man with a stick, both women with dogs. A senior citizens' patrol.

"There he is!" the man cried.

One of the two women screamed. One of the dogs began to yap. The other followed suit. The group had now reached the middle of the intersection. The man spread out his arms, using his stick as a barrier. *Don't do that*, Moses thought. And: *Hopefully, they aren't armed*. He started to run faster.

The other woman yelled: "Here! Help! Help!"

Past them into the T-crossing and down the next street. Moses could still hear one last "Hellllp!" with a very long L.

Dogs, Moses thought fleetingly. *Real dogs. They weren't here yet.* Keep running. Forward and to the right toward the river. Straight ahead and slightly downhill toward...Toward where? There were no directions. Everything here was off-limits, everything was cut off by an endless wall. Make up your mind.

Somewhere behind him, he heard the short yelp of a police siren. A guard appeared in front of him. So to the right it was. Free until the next T-intersection. Very close to the river. Then see from there. Run.

Moses couldn't see the guard who had hidden behind one of the walls. He was mid-stride with both feet off the ground when the body check came. Stumbled to the side, couldn't regain his balance, landed with his chest against a trash can that fell over. He somersaulted over the large plastic container and landed in the filth that was now spilling out of the can. The other man fell on top of him and kept rolling due to his momentum. The guard crashed into the wall of the next house with his shoulder and yelled loudly with pain.

But he was quickly back up on his feet, faster than Moses, who was still sliding around in the garbage. The security guy planted himself in front of him, legs spread, as he held his shoulder. Moses slowly stood up as the whee-ooo, whee-oo of the police siren grew closer. The guard was obviously in extreme pain as he cried: "Just stand there! They'll catch you!"

The police car rounded the corner. Moses turned around, slid precariously on the trash again, regained his balance, and sprinted across the street.

"Stop!" came the order from the police loudspeaker. "This is the police! Stop immediately."

Moses was just vaulting over a waist-high wall. As he took off, he noticed that something slimy was stuck to his shoe. He was lucky he hadn't face planted against the wall.

The police sped up, and as Moses slipped down the side

of the house, he could already hear the brakes. Doors opening, doors slamming, boots running. Moses was behind the
house, paused to consider his options, ran along the house
toward the neighboring yard instead of making a beeline for
the next street. A hedge with yellow flowers, thick but not
too tall. He dove across it and landed on the other side. A
soft impact this time. He hunched up small. Wanted to be
invisible. Once again. Forever now.

"Where is he?" he heard a man ask.

"Has to be back there," a woman said.

Back there meant not here in the front. They were looking
somewhere else. The voices soon moved away.

"Do you see him?" The man. Further off.

"Not here." The woman.

Moses looked around, but didn't stand up. Hanging in
the window, a poster of Itumeleng Khune. The Kaizer Chiefs'
goalie. And captain. Was he actually where he'd wanted to
be? The house had two stories, as he recalled. He got to his
feet and crouched over as he ran toward the front facade.
There was the tricot in the window. There was the mailbox
which had caused him to even notice the house in the first
place. Moses walked up to the front door and hoped to remain
out of sight until the door opened. He knocked and waited.

60 "We've never taken out anyone," Nozipho said
quietly. They were standing at the window and
looking out at the street.

"I know," Thembinkosi said.

"It isn't our style."

"I know."

"We do what we do because we're good at it. And not
the other."

Thembinkosi didn't say anything.

"And when that girl tried to steal my purse...you weren't
even able to hit her. I had to do it."

"I know. But we've always known that at some point it

might be necessary. And as far as that girl..."

"Psst!"

Footsteps could be heard in the hallway. It was too late to slip into the wardrobe. The steps kept going. Piss splashed in the toilet.

"I need to go, too," Nozipho said.

"As far as that girl was concerned, that was completely different. You didn't have to hit her."

"But I wanted to." Flushing.

"Good. You had a right to do it, I think," Thembinkosi said. "And here, we might not have any other choice."

"But what should we do? Smash him over the head with something?" Steps in the hallway. High Voice was going back to the lounge.

"If necessary."

"If so, you'll be the one doing it."

Outside, a police bakkie drove up, parking next to the one remaining security company Polo. Inter-vehicle communication. One man and one woman were sitting in the police vehicle.

"Shit," Thembinkosi said.

The security car started and drove off. The police truck followed. The street was free.

"Great!" Thembinkosi said.

The couple didn't say anything for a few moments.

"How are you going to do it?" Nozipho asked.

Thembinkosi didn't answer.

A young man ran down the street. In the other direction.

"There he is!" Thembinkosi said. "The guy from earlier." A guard hurried after him. "But how can he still be running around out there?" Nozipho asked.

The police vehicle trailed the guard. Flashers on. Sharp yelp of a siren.

"He's the cause of all this mess?" Nozipho said.

"Apparently."

"But they have to catch him eventually. He's just one against so many."

"True."

"What do you think he's done?"

"Rich people live around here. We're not the only ones interested in that fact."

"But the whole cavalry against one person who stole something?"

"Doesn't make sense to me either."

For a few seconds, it was peaceful both inside and out.

"Now's our best chance to get out of here, Thembi. We have to do something."

"You're right."

The security Polo rolled up again, stopping in the exact same spot it had been parked earlier.

"Shit!" Nozipho.

"We still have to figure out what to do. We can't stay here."

 61 "Home invasion, burglary, attempted rape, theft, assault, anything else...?" Warrant Officer Zolani Mafu glanced to the side.

"Aggravated assault," Police Sergeant Yolanda Baker corrected. "On top of that."

"Aggravated assault," Mafu repeated into the radio.

"How could anybody commit so many crimes in such a short time?" a voice crackled down the line. "Is the suspect armed?"

"No one knows." Mafu.

"How did he commit assault and aggravated assault?"

Mafu glanced at Baker. "Beat an old man and injured his wife with a chair. Broke the leg of a security guard when he tried to hold on to him."

"And the rape?"

"He broke into a house that belonged to the woman."

"With his haul?"

"Apparently." Baker looked at Mafu. He nodded.

"Then nab him. Reinforcements are on their way."

62 A TV was switched on in the lounge. Loud. Some show with a jeering audience.

"One thing's clear," Thembinkosi said. "We don't want to kill him, just incapacitate him. We want to get out of here, and he's in our way. But there's another problem."

"What?" Nozipho asked.

"Actually there are two problems..."

"We don't have any weapons?"

"That's the one. I also don't know how we can attack him."

"With our hands. There's two of us, only one of him."

"But what if he's prepared for something? If he has a gun on him? If he notices us before we reach him?"

Nozipho started to open the wardrobe doors, before crouching down and opening the dead woman's small suitcase. Underneath the clothes, she found a cosmetics bag and unzipped it. Rummaged around in it a little. Pulled out a nail file and held it up. "Women know how to defend themselves."

In the other room, High Voice was channel surfing. A sports show.

"What am I supposed to do with that?"

Nozipho pondered this for a second, then stood up, smoothed her dress, raised her arm, and stabbed the file downward a few times.

"That?" she asked.

"You want me to slaughter him?"

"I want to get out."

The two of them said nothing for a moment. The sports reporter was shouting enthusiastically.

"And what's the second problem?"

"He's just murdered a person, maybe more than one. Which means he isn't likely to just let us go. When he realizes that we're in the house, he'll do everything he can to make sure we're the ones who are knocked out."

"We won't both fit in the freezer."

"That's comforting. Although..." Thembinkosi said, looking

around. "As big as it is..."

63 No sounds from within the house. No footsteps, no calls of "Could you answer the door?" Moses looked around. Nobody in sight. No threat from the side.

He knocked one more time. Not too loudly, not too in- sistently. He didn't want to alarm the whole street, just the people in this house. In this one house. Somebody had to help him.

"No one's home." He heard a child's voice behind him.

Moses gave a start and spun around.

The girl was maybe eight years old. She was wearing a blue and black school uniform, her cornrows caught into a single braid down her back. She was carrying a writing case and a pen. "Busi is still at ballet, but her mom will pick her up soon. You'll have to wait."

She was his rescue! Wherever she was heading was where he wanted to go. A door that would open, that would also open to him. The face of an adoring mother who would also show him favor and respond to him with general phil- anthropic love. Black solidarity. Now the new South Africa would show itself to be more than just a constitution that nobody had ever read.

"Say," Moses began. "Would you like to play a game with me?" Even as he said this, he knew the question was inappropriate.

"Yeah!" the girl said. "What kind of game?"

Good. She wasn't yet leery of questionable activities.

"Tell me... Who's waiting on you at home?"

"Mommy!"

"Mommy. Super. The game...The game goes like this: We have to get home to your mommy without anyone seeing us."

The girl thought about this for a few seconds. Moses wondered if maybe she did know something about adults and their less-upstanding intentions. But then she glanced around and said: "Interesting."

"Does that mean, yes?"

"Sure!"

Moses dropped to the ground.

"Is this part of the game?"

"Yes," Moses said. He had just caught sight of a guard out of the corner of his eye. "We have to start right away. Follow me."

Moses crawled to the furthest corner of the little garden. The wall there was tall enough to conceal both of them.

The girl sprang after him like a puppy, laughing all the while.

"But we have to stay completely silent. Nobody, absolutely nobody, should know what we're doing."

"Oops!" she breathed, covering her mouth with her one free hand. She then crouched down behind the wall as well.

Moses raised his head and looked over the top of the wall. The guard, a young woman, was very diligently looking down the sides of each house. Thoroughly, but not too thoroughly. She was doing what she'd been ordered to do, no more, no less.

"A woman's coming," Moses told the girl. "She shouldn't see us."

"Okay," she answered, ducking down even further.

The young woman's footsteps were now quite audible. Tap, tap, each one a little louder. Her steps were measured, rhythmic. Tap, tap, the steps grew quieter.

"Good!" Moses said.

"Good!" the girl said.

"My name's Moses. What's yours?"

"Flower. What should we do now?"

"Now we'll go to your parents' house, without anyone seeing us."

"It's my mother's house. My father lives somewhere else. Mommy says he's a son of a bitch. But only when I'm not in the same room. What's a son of a bitch?"

"Uuuhhh," Moses stuttered. "Someone...Someone who doesn't love his wife, Flower."

"Hm!" she said, studying him skeptically.

Moses knew that he'd just given her a very pat answer, but he couldn't think of a better one. He slowly stood up and looked around.

"Are you the man they're all looking for?"

Moses' heart started racing.

"You can tell me. I won't tell anyone."

Moses gazed down at Flower and considered how he could explain his situation.

"Yes," he said. "I'm the one, but I haven't done what they're saying...It's not true."

"That's what I thought."

"Why?" Moses asked.

"You can tell, can't you?"

"You mean what they're saying I did?"

"Aunt Grace says you stole something. And you hurt people. Is that true?"

"Well, I didn't steal anything."

"What about hurting those people?"

"Only because they wanted to catch me."

"You didn't want to?"

"No."

"Then you were just defending yourself?"

"Yes. We really need to get out of here."

"Okay."

"How far is it to your house?

"Pretty far."

"Then let's get going."

 What a shitty stressful day. There'd been a fire in Palm Trees, and before the fire department could get there, the house's roof had collapsed. They'd been lucky that in this heat other houses hadn't caught on fire as well. The neighbors had dumped water on their own houses non-stop. When he'd asked one of them why he hadn't spared at least one bucket of water to toss on the fire, things had gotten out of hand. And now the mess in The Pines.

Warren Kramer opened the door to the monitor room. "What's going on?"

"They haven't caught him, Boss," Happiness said.

"How can that be? How many people are there now?"

"Six vehicles. Fifteen people. Even the Boss is there."

"Gerrit?"

"Yes, Boss van Lange."

"So why isn't it working? It can't be all that hard to catch that bastard. A tsotsi."

"I don't think so, Boss."

"That it should be easy to catch him?"

"That he's a tsotsi, Boss."

"Show him to me."

Happiness hit a couple of keys and zoomed in on the paused footage. "There, Boss."

Kramer saw scruffy rags. Too muscular and fit for those trashy clothes, but so what? Clothes made the man, after all. And the guy looked like shit. "What are the cameras showing now?"

Happiness searched for other images of the boy. Ran the footage from the four cameras backward.

"Stop!" Kramer said. "Who's that?"

With the press of one button, all four cameras stopped. "The two people there. Who are they?" An attractive man and a woman in a smock.

Happiness had never seen either one of them. But Boss Kramer shouldn't know that. "Two people," she said.

"Seen them before?"

"I think so," she said, although the two of them were complete strangers to her. She would've noticed and remembered the man. She watched the two for a while. Kramer gradually lost interest, as hers increased. Not because the man was so handsome, though. Something wasn't quite right about the way the two of them were behaving, though she had no idea what was bothering her. But they were chatting...as if they knew each other well. Really well. Only...why would a man in a fashionable suit and a domestic worker be on such friendly terms? Seem so familiar? Relaxed. Better not to say anything. She must have been watching other footage when they'd been out on the street. Or maybe asleep.

"They must've left a long time ago, don't you think?" the Boss asked.

"Must've," she agreed.

 Thembinkosi took the nail file from Nozipho. Stared at it. Raised his arm and jabbed it firmly into a body that wasn't there.

"What a crappy day!"

The sports commentator had worked himself into a frenzy. His voice kept cracking in excitement.

"Let's go," Nozipho said. "It's time." She reached for the doorknob.

"Wait. It's not that easy. What if he's standing on the other side of the door?"

"Then he's discovered us either way."

"But we have to be prepared, make a plan."

"The best plan is to surprise him."

"Can you have something to use, too?"

"Such as?"

"I don't know, whatever."

Outside, a car's brakes screeched. They heard High Voice run into the garage. The door opened. The car drove in.

"It's too late anyway," Thembinkosi said.

 "Come on," Flower said, grabbing Moses' hand. He didn't elude her grasp, though he knew the security guys would take him out if they saw this. Luckily, the girl dragged him over to a wall that was so high, she needed both hands to climb over it. She dropped his hand and led the way.

"You're still thinking that nobody should be able to see us, right?"

"Yeah." Flower paused at the street and looked around. "I'll cross first."

She left him where he was standing and crossed the street. After she reached the other side, she looked around once more before motioning at him.

Moses ran to catch up with her. Ducked behind the next wall. "How do you know your way around here so well?"

"Because of Busi. And my cousin Nandi, too. When she's here, they sometimes let us go outside on our own. My cousin's already twelve. Come on."

Flower studied the lay of the land like a burglar and crept through front yards, over terraces, and under hedges. Moses followed her until she came to a stop at a street. She raised a finger to her lips, then pointed back the way they had just come. Moses didn't understand immediately what she was trying to say. She pointed once more in the same direction as he heard footsteps. He finally understood and hid. He flattened himself behind a tree and heard a voice he recognized.

"Flower, you're being a naughty little girl again!" The referee. Flower giggled. "You know very well you aren't allowed to play here."

"I'm about to go."

"I should tan your heinie." Lecherous pig.

"I'm going, promise." Flower's voice was already fading.

"I'll be watching you," the referee called after her.

Silence. They had reached a part of The Pines that Moses didn't recognize. Closer to the road from Abbotsford to Dorchester Heights. However, this did him no good if he couldn't climb over the wall. Maybe it was at least good that they wouldn't be looking for him here.

"Moses!" Flower was back.

"What do you actually play with Busi and Nandi?"

"We hide so they can't see us." When Moses didn't say anything, she continued: "We aren't allowed to play here.

All this is private property, but we do it anyway. We just have to make sure nobody sees us."

Cool girl. If she develops other interests later on, I could fall in love with her, Moses thought.

"Back there," she pointed toward the river, "are two cars. The people in them are wearing uniforms. And over there," she pointed in the opposite direction, "I saw a police car drive by. It didn't head this way, though. And then I saw old Mrs. Peacock, but she doesn't say anything."

"Why doesn't she say anything?"

"She can't."

"Did she have a stroke?"

"Tongue cancer."

"How do you know that?"

"From Nandi. She heard it from her mother. And she heard it from Mommy."

"She doesn't have a tongue anymore?"

Flower shook her head. "Come on. We gotta go."

"How far is it?"

"We still have to cross two more streets."

 Nozipho was still gripping the bedroom doorknob. Thembinkosi was leaning against the door as he held the nail file away from his body. They were staring at each other.

"Do you have the money?" High Voice. Thembinkosi reached for Nozipho's hand.

"Why would I?"

"It's gone."

"What do you mean, it's gone?"

"It's no longer where I stuck it." High Voice was growing louder.

"Where did you put it?"

"In one of the drawers. Here. In the kitchen." The scraping of boots. Drawers opening and shutting.

"You're joking."

"No, I swear."

"But the old woman can't have the money. She was dead by the time you hid it."

"I know."

"Then explain it to me." Deep Voice was growing quieter with each sentence. Neither of them said a word. "Explain it to me."

"Someone was in the house."

"That's ridiculous. Who would come in here?"

"But.. the ID. It's missing, too."

Deep Voice began to walk up and down, slowly at first, then faster. Stopped. Resumed pacing.

"What will they do?" Nozipho mouthed silently.

"Kill each other."

"Or tear up the apartment."

Thembinkosi thought about the slip. And the shirts. And the dress Nozipho was wearing. The empty hangers.

"What is it?" High Voice asked. He sounded frightened. "Spit it out!" The boots stopped. "I'm thinking."

"We should get back in the wardrobe." Nozipho.

"How could someone get in here?" Deep Voice.

"Come on." Nozipho.

"Wait." Thembinkosi.

"We didn't activate the alarm." High Voice.

"You didn't activate the alarm." Deep Voice. "It's your house."

"Yes, my house, but it wasn't activated." High Voice.

"Come on!" Nozipho.

"No." Thembinkosi. "Be quiet!"

"Come on!" Deep Voice.

"Now!" Nozipho.

Thembinkosi wrapped his arms around Nozipho and held her tightly. Footsteps in the hallway. "Are you very sure?" Deep Voice.

"Definitely." High Voice sounded relieved.

"I want to take one last look in that fucking freezer."

Nozipho slipped out of Thembinkosi's arms. A few seconds

later both of them had vanished into the wardrobe again.

 68 Warrant Officer Henrik Bezuidenhout was standing at the entrance to The Pines as the bakkie with
the K9 unit finally drove up. Perhaps the problem would be
resolved shortly. It couldn't be all that difficult to catch a
young fugitive inside a well-secured and supervised gated
community and to hand him over to the law. In other words,
to him. At the moment, he was the highest-ranking cop on
site.

The vehicle was waved through and came to a stop. Jay-
Jay Dlomo stepped out.

"Nkosi's the best," he said. "He'll catch the guy in no time
at all."

The dog leaped out of the cage in the small Chevy.
Bezuidenhout watched as Dlomo ran his hand across the
German shepherd's head. The dog panted, stretching his long
tongue into the sunshine. Dlomo had been the first black
dog handler in East London. A good man. Two generations
of tsotsis had fled panic-stricken in front of his dogs. Sure,
they had shot a couple of his dogs. But in order to flee from
such a beast, you had to be fairly cold-blooded to not only
pull but fire a pistol. And hit your mark.

"Where all has the guy been?" Dlomo asked.

"What he's mainly done is run from everyone."

"And always gotten away?"

"Uh-huh."

"Amateurs! That won't happen to us, will it?" Dlomo patted
the dog.

"We heard that he's been inside at least two homes. One
of them was empty, but he grabbed some stuff there. And at
the other...a woman was at home. She was asleep when the
guy suddenly materialized beside her bed. He then tried to
rape her. When she screamed, he ran off. Wait a second."
Bezuidenhout studied a piece of paper. "I think the woman
ran over to a friend's house to calm down. The other house

is probably the easiest to start with. Someone's there now. An old man."

"How long was he in there?"

"Long enough to find the valuables and pocket them."

"Ah, that'll be enough for us. Right, my boy?" Dlomo looked down at his dog.

"I have the address here. Want to follow me?" Bezuidenhout asked.

 69 Flower was already on the other side of the street, and she gave the signal. Thumbs up.

Moses still looked around cautiously before sprinting across the street and crouching behind the next wall.

"This house is empty," Flower said. Moses saw closed curtains and a weathered facade.

"The person here died," Flower said. "And now no one wants to live here."

"Simply died?"

"I think so. Old people do that."

"Old people do do that. Sure. Are there many empty houses around here?"

"Yes. Mommy says some of them use automatic lights just to make other people think they're at home. Are you coming?"

They walked around the empty house.

"Now we have to be careful," Flower said.

"Why?"

"A witch lives there."

"Why would you think that?"

"Mommy says so."

"Why does she say that?"

"I don't know, but she's right. Whenever we're around here, she sees us."

"Does she live alone?"

They were now standing in front of the house. No curtains. Grimy windows. Withered grass.

"Yes. Otherwise she wouldn't always be looking out the window."

"Do you think she's at home right now?"

"She's always at home."

"Why is she a witch?" Moses couldn't see anyone at the windows. But perhaps the woman was looking out on the other side of the house.

"Because she always calls someone."

"Who?"

"I don't remember."

"The police?"

"I don't think so. I think she calls the other people who drive around in uniforms."

"And then? Do they come?"

"No."

"Why not?"

"Because no one believes her anymore. That's what Mommy says. Because they all know she's a witch."

Moses stopped listening. Mommy and the witch? It would take a little time to think through all this and figure it out. But he wasn't going to be able to pull that off right now. He was too tired.

And Flower still had a lot to learn.

70 Jay-Jay Dlomo followed his white colleague. *At his age,* he thought, *I was still seeing them set dogs on black people. Just for being black. Times had changed*, he thought. Who knew that better than he did?

The warrant officer's Nissan rounded a corner, then another one. It slowed down and stopped in front of a house. The door of a Central Alert car opened, and a young woman stepped out. She straightened her uniform and waited for something to happen. *The security people always talked a blue streak*, Dlomo thought. *But when the real police showed up, they knew their place.*

A haggard old man appeared at the front door. Shirt and

pants dangling off him like XXL-sized clothes on a starving child. He was carrying a little dog and slowly approached the newcomers. The dog nervously bobbed its head.

"Do you have him?" he asked. "Do you have my things?"

Dlomo saw Bezuidenhout shake his head and opened the tailgate of his truck.

"Nkosi, come!"

The German shepherd jumped down, snuffled the wind and ground, and then sat down beside Dlomo. Raised his head, waiting on a signal. Bezuidenhout nodded in their direction.

"It's been over thirty minutes since he was here. That shouldn't be a problem, right?" The warrant officer didn't wait for an answer. "This is Mr. Foster. Money and jewelry are missing. Can we go right inside? Mr. Foster, show us where the burglar was."

"He was everywhere in the house," the old man said. As he said this, the slack skin under his jaw quivered. "I'm sure he thought I wouldn't notice anything. But something was wrong with the lock, and then I saw that the...What is it?"

He looked down at the little dog he was carrying, which was staring at his larger cousin, his fur standing up in tufts. Nkosi hadn't even deigned to look at the little dog.

"And then?" Bezuidenhout urged. "May we come in?"

"There," Foster said as he walked into the bedroom. "I immediately noticed that. The doily on the dresser. It wasn't lined up with the edge."

"What's in the dresser?" Bezuidenhout.

"You should ask: What was in the dresser?" Foster.

"Fine. What was inside?"

"Money."

"How much?"

Foster hesitated for a second. Dlomo could already smell the lie in advance.

"25,000 rand."

"That's a lot of money for a dresser." Bezuidenhout.

"And here, you can see the doily. That's where it was

sitting. My sister brought it back for me from Australia."

The thing looked like a little rug. Dlomo had no idea why anyone would bring that back as a present.

"So, the burglar was definitely in here?" Bezuidenhout.

"Absolutely."

The warrant officer turned around. "What does the dog need now?"

"Something that the burglar held. Let's try that thing on the dresser." Dlomo picked up the rug and held it out for Nkosi to sniff. "Search," he said.

The dog sniffed at it for a few seconds and took a step toward Foster.

"Good, Nkosi," Dlomo said. "Not him."

The dog snuffled the rug a little more and picked up another scent. He dropped his nose to the floor, found something, and followed the trail. Dlomo let him lead the way. Nkosi entered every room in the house, turned around, caught a secondary trail, hesitated for a moment, and finally stopped at the front door. He barked once.

Now we're off, Dlomo thought.

71 "That's our house," Flower said. She pointed across the next street. Two stories, burgundy curtains, several windows open. A new compact car parked in front of the garage.

"That's Mommy's car?" Moses asked.

"Uh-huh...Come on, we'll go over there."

"Wait a minute."

The two of them were hidden behind a wall over which Flower could just barely see. Moses looked up and down the street. Over toward the exit, he heard a garbage truck— or was it driving on the road that ran outside The Pines? The road leading down to the river was empty. Although... A security vehicle was just turning down the street. It was the bakkie that had tried to run him down. Or it might be a different one identical to the other one. *Stay calm,* Moses told himself. The most critical thing was to get to safety. And safety was only a few meters away on the other side of the street.

The bakkie slowly drew closer. Moses knelt down and let it drive by. As the sound of the motor died away, he stood up.

"Now!" he said to Flower.

A few seconds later, she rang the doorbell. At first, there was no reaction from inside the house. A window was then shut somewhere. Footsteps. Stairs. Now they were coming closer.

A woman opened the door. Slender face, red glasses, hair smooth to her shoulders. Black t-shirt and jeans. Not stupid. The smile on her lips morphed into a what-the-fuck look when she saw who was standing behind her daughter. For a long time, she didn't say anything. But just as Moses was about to start his explanation, she rediscovered her voice.

"Get in the house!" she ordered Flower, who turned around and gazed into Moses' eyes.

She then walked around Mommy, but looked back one last time. "But Moses hasn't done anything," she said.

"Go!" Mommy insisted. "Go to your room." Up the stairs, door open, door closed.

Mommy stood in the middle of the doorframe. She wasn't especially tall, but she made an intimidating impression on Moses as her eyes bored into his. She slowly placed her hands on her hips.

"I just need help," Moses said quietly.

"If you ever get close to my daughter again..."

"But..."

"You're the one everyone's looking for, right? I know what you did. They'll catch you. You can bet on that."

She slammed the door.

"But..." Moses tried once more.

He glanced around. The street was empty, but it wouldn't be for long. He needed a new plan. Where was Sandi? Had she even come?

A knock over his head. Flower was standing at a second-floor window, waving sadly. Moses waved back. He felt just as sad.

Flower spun around suddenly. Mommy must have just come in the room. He had to get out of here.

 72 The garage door shut again. Footsteps heading straight into the room.

"But I took the money out." High Voice.

"Look one more time." Deep Voice.

Thembinkosi listened while someone sat down on the bed and opened the suitcase zipper. Rummaged around. Threw things on the floor.

"I told you it's not in there." High Voice.

Thembinkosi could see his shadow through the cracks in the wardrobe louvers. High Voice was sitting less than a meter from the door. He tried to hold his breath.

"Then tell me where it is." Deep Voice was now very quiet.

"I don't know." High Voice's voice grew a little higher.

"I'm not saying you have it, but I'd like to know you're giving some thought to this. Tell me what you think."

"How do you mean that?"

For a few moments, Thembinkosi heard nothing. Deep Voice then inhaled and exhaled, loudly and slowly. "Look, I just want to know what happened. What did you do with the money?"

"You know that already. I put it in the kitchen drawer."

Another pause. Deep Voice was waiting for High Voice to continue. "And?" he finally prodded.

"And?... It's gone now." Pause. A long one.

"Explain that."

"I can't."

Outside the sound of cars driving up. Doors slamming.

"Give it a try. Just a little one."

"Shit," High Voice said.

"What?"

"Out there. The dog."

"They're not here because of us." Deep Voice's voice grew even quieter. It sounded menacing.

Silence. Again. Thembinkosi tried to imagine what was going on outside the house. Cars. Sure. A dog? Why?

"Someone was here," High Voice now said. Silence. Another second and then another. And then another.

Open the wardrobe door, apologize for being in the wrong place at the wrong time. We just want to get out of here, just want to go home. Best of luck with the corpse! And, uh...by the way, here's the money. No hard feelings. None at all!

Still silence. Deep Voice eventually broke it. "Exactly."

High Voice leaped up. Some synapse had finally fired. "You think I'm the one behind it!"

"Did I say that?"

"No, but..."

Shit, thought Thembinkosi. If this were a film, they would now be at each other's throats.

If this were a film, nobody would be standing in the wardrobe. Unbelievable.

"Did you tell anyone about it?"

"You."

"Anyone else?"

"No, of course not."

"Who could've known then?"

"Nobody."

"Could someone have suspected? Gwen?"

"How? She hears us plan to murder her mother? We set the trap for her, and Gwen lets us do it and then comes to the house to grab the money out from under us?"

"And your mother-in-law herself?"

"She's dead. She couldn't have taken the money." High Voice was growing more self-assured. Receding fear. Deep Voice wouldn't take him out. At least, not immediately.

"But she might have told someone. My son-in-law says he's in trouble, but I don't believe him."

"And someone followed her?"

"Why not?"

"And waits until she's dead to take the money."

"What did you actually tell her?"

"You know already."

"I wasn't there."

"They've left again," High Voice said. He began to pace up and down.

"What?" Silence.

"Oh! The dog and the people. They're gone." High Voice. "I told her that I didn't know what to do. And I told her about the Czech."

"So, the truth."

"Yes, just not the amount. I exaggerated that. A little."

"That was the plan. What did you tell her about the Czech?"

"The truth, that he's going to kidnap Gwen, and then rape her and cut her into little pieces."

"If he didn't get his money back."

"Yes. If he didn't get his money back."

 Leaden legs. Moses turned back toward the street with the thought that he would never again run as long as he lived. There was no point to any of this here. What had he run away from in the first place? A poor white man who hadn't accepted the political transition. A caretaker whose responsibility it was to repair faucets. A couple of security guards who didn't understand the difference between democracy and dictatorship. They were stuck in jobs that had no real productive value as it was.

Pull yourself together, he admonished himself. Everyone was just doing their job, just trying to survive. Except for the white guy with the club. And then there were the cops. They were after him, too.

He didn't want to run anymore.

Looked down the street to the right. Empty. Left. Empty.

How in the world was he supposed to get out of here?

One more glance to the right. Shit. The white man with the club. And he had already caught sight of him.

So to the left. A security car was now driving toward him. The same bakkie again.

Moses turned around and ran. Past Flower's house to the wall, and then left down the hill. Toward the exit. However, a guard was standing in the yard a few houses down. With his back to him, yelling something or other. Had to have seen him.

Moses whipped back around, running back the way he'd come. Once again the wrong way. Away from the exit. Away from rescue. Away from Sandi. Was she on her way yet?

74 Ludelwa Tontsi was still standing next to the Central Alert car when the dog sniffed the threshold. She was thinking about her mother and what she had advised her. Better to have a badly paid job than none at all. And it was indeed badly paid. She received 2,200 rand for an entire month of work. Six days a week, twelve hours a day. After deducting the 300 rand for the shack in Duncan Village and the cost of the taxi trips to the headquarters, she barely had enough to pay for food. Bread, milk, and instant oatmeal for breakfast…And she could forget about a monthly visit to her family in Mnyameni. Those 150 kilometers also came at a price. That was why she had to sometimes ask her mother to send her money, so that she could pay for the trip out of her pension.

Now the dog was coming out of the house, the black cop right behind him. Then the white cop. The old man who owned the house stayed at the door.

Her phone rang. She glanced at the screen. The junior boss. She took the call.

"Ludelwa?"

"Mmhm." Of course, it was her. He had called her after all.

"You're still at the house of that old…Mr.—what's his name?—Foster?"

"Yes."

"The dog's there?"

"They're coming out now."

"Good. I'd like you to stay with them. Whenever something happens, I want us to be there." Stevie van Lange hesitated. "Okay? I don't want the cops to later say we weren't there to help."

"Okay," Ludelwa said.

"All right, so stick with them." Van Lange hung up.

Her mother had given her one more piece of advice when she'd gotten started. When a job is so poorly paid, always wait until someone tells you what to do. Forget about showing initiative. That's why you have superiors. Ludelwa had always followed that advice.

The dog led the way, the two cops behind him. They didn't say a word. Ludelwa wondered fleetingly if she should follow them on foot. She decided to get into the car and follow them at walking speed.

The white cop looked over his shoulder when he realized that she was behind them. The other one just watched the dog. The animal had its nose to the ground and rounded a corner onto a street leading to the right. It then hesitated and retraced its steps as if it had made a mistake. The dog stopped, turned around again, and went down the street after all.

Now the dog seemed to be more confident. A hundred meters in front of her, she could see another company car. The dog walked up to it and stopped. The two cops exchanged glances, then greeted whoever was in the Central Alert vehicle. Ludelwa couldn't tell who was at the wheel.

For a few seconds, time seemed to stand still. Just like the dog, which was standing like a statue. Like the two cops, who were waiting for the dog to do something. The animal then turned and took a few steps toward one of the houses. Stopped again.

The dog now started to bark loudly. It was probably too hot for him.

75 Moses vaulted over the waist-high hedge. *Too much effort, too much strength*, he thought. He didn't need to jump so high. However, he also didn't want to fall again. Lawn, small walls, a bed, lawn, another hedge. Falling down meant losing time. And getting hurt.

Everything was pointless. He hadn't done anything. Another low wall, grass with flowers, children's toys, a wide bed, a long jump, over the next hedge, as well. Something with thorns. Just don't get tangled up. Just don't fall. Okay... the two houses. The security guy with the leg. And the other with the...he didn't want to think about it. The kick between his legs must have hurt horribly.

At the thought of what he could have done with that kick, Moses felt sick. Up ahead, a sharp bend in the wall because he had reached the Nahoon again. As far away from the exit as he could possibly be. He stopped for a second. Turning around, he saw the guard was on his trail but moving slowly. From somewhere, a police siren was coming closer. He heard a second one further off. A dog was barking its head off. Far away. He wiped the sweat off his face and glanced down at himself. His pants were torn and filthy. Luckily, he had put on his Adidas this morning. It was still too hot for them, but they had kept him from slipping when hauling around the boxes. Now he was glad to have on shoes that he could run in. His t-shirt had weathered everything amazingly well. A few spots, dirt, sweat, a tear. His lower arms were dirty. He tried to wipe them on his jeans. Again. The siren grew closer.

Only two more yards until the 90-degree angle, then along the river. Somewhere, he thought, there had to be a way out of this repeating loop. Run, get away, get found, run, get away. At some point. *Soon,* he added. *Otherwise, they'll catch me.* There were already so many of them, and their numbers kept increasing.

Another hedge, a lawn, slow down a little to round the corner, speed back up. Ugh, this wall was really tall. A good launch, cleared it, landed, briefly off-balance, caught himself, keep going.

He didn't see a thing. It came out of nowhere. An attack like in a war. He was just tensing up to take the next leap as his lower body was ripped apart. There was nothing he could do about it. There was the one movement, which was his, and there was the other, which came from somewhere else. And it was much stronger.

It knocked him over, and he tumbled across the lawn, barely missing hitting his head against a skateboard and landing in topsoil. Face first.

His relief to have not broken anything lasted less time than it took lightning to strike a tree. What landed on top of Moses was heavy and grunting.

"Bastard!"

Moses felt the air being squeezed out of him. The thing on his back punched him.

"Bastard!" Then again. "Always knew we'd get you. You can't get out."

As Moses tried to catch his breath, bare arms and legs wrapped around him. *Shit,* he thought. The referee.

The arms were workers' arms, sturdy and muscular. What they lacked in flexibility, they made up for in sheer strength. The legs were wrapped around his own. Now he could breathe, but he couldn't move even a little.

The sirens were nearby. One of them had stopped somewhere.

They were both lying on their sides. The referee's fist was punching his chest, while his legs tightened more and more. How old was the man? Had to be almost retirement age. He wasn't agile, but Moses still couldn't move a centimeter. How was he supposed to get away? As soon as the others got here, he'd be done for.

Moses recalled his earlier train of thought in regards to the police. No hope there. He tried again to move.

An arm. A little. Hopeless. The other. No chance.

His legs. Something had to work.

Behind him, the referee growled: "Just wait. God has a plan for each one of us. Yours is prison."

No! Moses thought. Only one part of his body was relatively free, a part that the referee had no way to control. *You could use your head for more than thinking,* Moses thought. He took a deep breath, as somewhere very, very close, tires squealed. The guard he'd seen a few moments before couldn't be far away, either. *Now or never,* he told himself. He bent his head as far forward as possible. He was now lying half on his side, half on his stomach. His forehead pressed into the dry bed, and he pushed as far as he could until he felt resistance. He took two seconds to focus.

And then threw his head back as hard as he possibly could. A loud crack. Penetrating. Then a throbbing pain in his head.

"Ow!" he heard the referee cry.

The man immediately released him, both top and bottom. Moses pulled free from the slack arms and legs.

Dampness down his back. The referee's blood. He had hit his mark.

As he stood up, he saw the man stretched out on the ground. He was in pain, and his nose was bleeding as if someone had sliced it off. Moses reached for the back of his head where it hurt, although he was aware which of the two of them was suffering more. He felt sorry for the man, knew how unnecessary this was. Now the referee started to whimper. All his strength was gone, all his confidence.

Get it together, Moses urged himself. *He wouldn't waste any time on you. Get out of here.*

Now! Immediately!

Moses couldn't. His legs were numb. Voices came from behind the corner of the outer wall. Low, but animated.

His watch was broken. A crack in the face. He could still see what time it was. 2:36.

His legs had to obey. He hurled himself over the next wall and crawled more than he ran to the next one. Hauled himself over that one as well, and collapsed. He was completely drained.

From where he hid, he saw two guards bend down to inspect the referee.

Keep going, Moses.

 "Who else has a key?"

"No one."

"Think."

"There's the management," they heard High Voice say. "Someone there probably has a key. A copy. We rented this from them."

"The house doesn't belong to you?"

"No, to people who work somewhere abroad. Saudi Arabia. Or Afghanistan. The Pines' management office handles the rental."

"Incredible."

"I'm just saying."

Silence. Nobody said anything. No footsteps. Thembinkosi almost burst in the wardrobe. It was so hot. He was drenched in sweat. If only they would keep talking.

"I really don't have it."

"If I believed that..."

"What?"

"Nothing."

Outside, a dog began to bark.

"And when does the Czech want the money?"

"The day after tomorrow."

"In the restaurant?"

"Uh-huh."

"Why did you have to open a restaurant anyway? What a lousy idea."

The dog didn't stop.

 As Nkosi started barking and then refused to stop, Meli was just in the process of trimming the small jasmine bush. He had to do everything slowly in order to fill his work hours, so he was devoting himself to his task with great passion. He had to find things to do until four o'clock, at which point he could knock on Mrs. Viljoen's door and tell her that he was done for the day. The dog was barking incessantly. Meli decided it must have something to do with all the security guards and cops. But he didn't know precisely what. It also had nothing to do with him. Everyone wearing a uniform looked down on him anyway.

Bismarck van Vuuren was lurking behind a bend in a wall that symbolically separated two properties. He didn't know exactly why the dog had started barking like crazy. The boy was actually close by, and that was why the dog had been brought—to find him. But he had managed to find him himself. And had decided to save time by cutting through this way instead of chasing after him. The boy was much faster anyway. He'd soon catch him though. He just had to wait. He could already see him.

As Nkosi wore himself out, Sandi was standing in a back-yard in Southernwood, far away from The Pines.

"You can take it as it is," said Sy, the cousin of a friend. "It's not exactly new, but you can see that. I bought it like this and don't know what I'll do with it. Great deal. You'll need to gas it up," Sy added. "And bring it back just like it is."

Jay-Jay Dlomo hadn't seen Nkosi bark like this all that often. *In the end*, he thought, *dogs aren't people, and you can't read their minds* But who could do that with a person either? He placed a hand on the animal's head and hoped this would calm it back down. The dog had done his job. The fugitive was probably hidden in the house. He saw Bezuidenhout on his phone, probably calling for backup. His job was now done. He just needed to calm Nkosi back down, and then he could head out. But the dog just kept barking. He'd never known him to act like this.

"Dad, what are we doing?"

"We'll catch him soon. Mark my words."

"Okay...but it's taking a long time. And we have...wait...

six cars there and, just a sec...twelve people, not counting you. We need them other places."

"Thanks for reminding me of that. That's just what I need right now."

"Sorry, Dad. You're there. But what are we doing?... Dad?"

"Wait. The dog started barking. The police requested he be brought here. I'll go check it out and call you back soon."

Flower was afraid of dogs, but she knew instinctively that she wanted to be outside right now. He was barking at another house somewhere. Did it have something to do with Moses? She considered climbing out her window, but Mommy would be back upstairs in a few minutes, wanting her to eat her fruit salad. That would cause trouble. He wasn't stopping, the dog.

Willie heard the dog. It had been barking for at least a minute, if not longer. He was once again in the wrong place, but all he had to do now was follow the barking. Maybe there would be a chance to be useful. A minor heroic act on the sidelines. The black boy might try to run, and he would stop him. And then, van Lange, that arrogant asshole, would finally offer him a job. What he really wanted to do was shoot the boy in the head. It had been a long time since he'd taken down any blacks.

Mrs. Viljoen was watching Meli when the dog began to bark. You always had to keep an eye on them. And that bush over there... he was trimming it so irritatingly slowly that she was thinking about docking him ten of the hundred rand she'd have to pay him shortly.

"Madam," he always said after he knocked on the door. "I'm done." At least he waited outside. Not like the last man, who had always stepped right inside even though he didn't have a right to be in there. Well, he'd get his hundred rand. Even if it was only because of the respect he showed her. That dog...What was going on?

Warren Kramer stuck his hand out of the car and greeted the Central Alert man who was standing by the entrance to

The Pines. People knew him here. "Any news?" he asked.

"I haven't heard much out here," the guard said. He was fit and was sweating profusely. A female colleague in uniform was sitting in the wall's shadow. She jumped up as she caught sight of the junior boss. Somewhere far away, a dog started to bark. All three listened to it. The barking didn't stop.

"Where is that?" Kramer asked.

The male guard gestured vaguely into The Pines. "Police dog. Just got here. That went fast...I mean, if they've caught him that is."

"I'll drive over there and take a look." Kramer tried to follow the barking as he drove into the gated community. Maybe this had been a wasted trip.

"Work faster, chaps!" Rob van der Merwe was standing in the shade of a scrawny little tree, thinking about the fact they still had one last job to do that afternoon. Nothing major, but it was in Amalinda, a few kilometers away. The commuter traffic would be starting soon, and they still had a solid hour of work to finish here. They'd get it done somehow, even if the boys had to work overtime. "Hurry up!"

A dog nearby began to bark. Deep barks, just like his Rhodesian Ridgeback, a marvelous animal. You could depend on a dog like that. And they were so quiet. However, if someone trespassed on his farmland, Bobby could make things quite uncomfortable. But the dog here was anything but quiet. How did the neighbors put up with that? And he wouldn't stop barking. Van der Merwe grew curious. There'd be trouble. The dog had to be close by. He would take a look. Clapped his hands once more. "Chaps, smoke break! Ten minutes, then everyone back on task. And Mcebisi... you can go search for your bandana. Are you sure you had it when we drove in here?"

The black cop was kneeling beside the dog as Ludelwa got out of the car. She wanted to talk to her colleague in the other Central Alert vehicle. Watching the old man's place seemed safer to her than waiting here with the men for the hunt for the boy to continue. She rapped at the driver's door. She didn't know the man at the wheel, but the company employed so many people, this wasn't unusual. The man was older than her and heavy. He didn't even look at her when he spoke. "We should wait here. Reinforcements are coming." *He spoke good English*, Ludelwa thought. *And he wasn't a Xhosa.*

Happiness couldn't hear Nkosi's barking because all she had access to was a silent video stream. She didn't even suspect that the dog was barking. The images she was monitoring didn't cover the area where he had come to a stop. However, one thing puzzled her. Her impression had been that the boy she had just seen was actually located over toward the river. Only a short clip. He'd dashed through the picture—maybe he'd known that a camera was mounted there. But all the security guards and cops were currently moving around the center of The Pines. There had to be a reason for that. For just a moment, she'd considered calling Warren or the young van Lange. However, there was a reason for everything. Of that she was certain.

As Nkosi started to bark, Police Inspector Vukile Pokwana was driving his Citi Golf around the last traffic circle before Dorchester Heights. He'd almost driven into the curb, since he'd been driving with only one hand. No power steering here. The vehicle had been the only one available, but it was had been a better choice than his own car, since it was at least recognizable as a police vehicle. He had a bad feeling about what he was heading into. "I'm almost there, yes," he confirmed into his phone, as he struggled to keep the VW in its lane. "And I've asked the station in Cambridge to send us more manpower. There's no way this idiot's going to waste our entire day...Uh-huh...Like I said, I'm almost there."

Fucking dog. Warrant Officer Bezuidenhout turned aside and covered his ears. He needed to think. The boy was in this house, and since the dog wouldn't stop barking, he had to be aware that they were on to him. Storming the house was one possibility. Another was to demand that he come out. And to call in backup so nothing went wrong. Another security vehicle came around the corner and pulled up. The situation fell way beyond the scope of the security guys' responsibilities. Had he even loaded his service pistol? He pulled it from his holster to check. That fucking dog.

78 Already another hedge, already another wall. Moses jumped and ran. He knew he had to get away from the wall. If he didn't, the guards who had found the referee would easily spot him. And who knew...if one of them was carrying a service pistol...

Moses leaped to the side, ran a few steps toward the street, and hunched down. In front of him, a waist-high wall and a sightline deep into the middle of the gated community. Too much activity. He was looking down a street heading away from him. He saw the backs of two guards jogging in the opposite direction. A silver-and-blue Central Alert vehicle approached, before turning and following them down the street. A compact car drove up from his left. Hopefully, it wasn't going to park next to him. One, two, three...The car kept going. Just as the car turned into another driveway, a police car materialized. It also turned down the street that led into the center of The Pines.

The two guards who had just been helping the referee also showed up. They were supporting him with linked arms. His face was bleeding, his blue t-shirt was red, he looked old. The three of them were moving slowly. One of the two—the heavy one that hadn't been able to chase him—was on the phone. He could hear his voice, but couldn't make out what he was saying.

What could've happened? Why didn't they seem to care about him anymore? What could be worse than a young black man guilty of both theft and rape? More precisely: Who?

Now he could hear: "...the manager...They're coming now ... good...got away from me, too...the pig...we almost..."

Moses had no idea what the guard was talking about. The dog was barking like crazy. Wasn't stopping. He then heard a very different sound. And although he knew these things always sounded different on TV and in the movies... He knew it was a shot.

Moses waited for what would happen next. He then heard another. And yet another.

The three men were now standing right in front of him. "He's now shooting at us, too," the fat man said.

79 The two mem in the room were very quiet. The dog outside wasn't. He was yapping like there was no tomorrow. Thembinkosi was drenched in sweat, and all he wanted was to get out. Out of the wardrobe, out of the room, out of the house, out of the gated community.

They really needed to consider if they wanted to continue doing this. After today.

"What's it mean?" High Voice's voice almost cracked. "Look, that dog's barking at our house. What for?"

"I don't know." Deep Voice was as quiet as usual, but he was starting to stretch out his words. Thembinkosi could feel the tension in each one.

"But what does the dog want here? Why did they even bring it here?"

"Be quiet. Very quiet. Do you understand? I don't want you to say anything else. Not a sound, not a word. Can you manage that?"

"But...I mean..."

"Not a word!" Deep Voice was barely audible. That was how much his voice had dropped.

"Okay."

The dog was barking incessantly.

"Out there," Deep Voice whispered. "Something's not right."

"That's what I was saying."

"And I told you to keep your mouth shut!" They hadn't

heard Deep Voice speak so loudly.

"Okay."

"The dog can't help it. It's followed a scent. And the scent has led it here. It can't have anything to do with us. You may say something now. Fine by me. Say something if you want to contradict me."

High Voice said nothing.

"Good."

There was a flurry of activity outside. The dog kept barking. Cars pulled up. Doors slammed. Thembinkosi heard voices that were increasingly frantic. The dog stopped.

"Finally," High Voice breathed.

The dog started up again. All he'd done was take a breath.

"Shit," High Voice said. The dog barked continuously.

"Shit!" High Voice repeated.

But it sounded different somehow. Not as fatalistic as before. Not resigned. Not as a commentary on something everyone had known and seen for a long time.

"Shit!" he said again. And his tone changed from excitement to panic.

"Forget it!" Deep Voice urged.

"But look!"

"But he hasn't seen us. Forget it!"

"That's a pistol. He's holding a pistol."

"I can see it's a pistol, but that still doesn't have anything to do with us." Deep Voice was trying to stay cool, which he was managing to do with effort. "Put. That. Thing. Up."

"I won't let them take me out."

From what Thembinkosi had understood, someone outside was pointing a gun at the house. And one or two meters away from his hiding place, someone else was aiming at that same person. He had to do something. Anything.

"Put it away."

"You've ordered me around long enough." Footsteps moving around. Someone leaping. Someone falling.

"Stop it."

"See that?"

"We have to consider how to get out of here."

Thembinkosi opened his wardrobe door. He didn't say anything.

High Voice was standing with gun in hand over Deep Voice. High Voice was the skinny man with blonde curls that had seen too much sun. Faded jeans, gray polo shirt, sneakers. Deep Voice was more powerfully built, no gun in sight.

Bald head, white t-shirt with an ocean wave on it, darker jeans, leather shoes. He hadn't imagined the two of them so shabby.

They hadn't imagined that someone was in the wardrobe.

High Voice pointed his gun at Thembinkosi. Deep Voice sprang up and grabbed his arm.

High Voice fired.

The bullet shattered the window.

After the shot and the crashing glass, total silence descended for a second. Maybe a little longer. Even the dog didn't make a sound.

Then the silence ended again.

 It was like a bad bit of dialogue. First the one shot, then the next, followed by a third after the same time span. And then everyone was talking at the same time. Moses had gotten caught in a shootout once that had escalated at a gas station. A robbery gone wrong. Everyone in close proximity had taken cover as best they could. By the end, the four thieves, two cops and two schoolchildren were lying dead on the pavement. He'd never forget that. Above all, because he'd been caught in the middle of it all. He had hidden under one of the delivery vans, hoping its gas tank wouldn't be hit. The day that he'd come the closest to dying.

But that wasn't anything like this situation. Back then he'd been lying under the delivery van, listening to the burst of individual gun shots. This time he could hardly distinguish one shot from the other.

The three men had immediately thrown themselves onto the ground. Even the referee, who had just needed support to walk, found a new lease on life in the moment he thought he might die. It took a few seconds for the three of them to realize that the gunfire was some distance away from them. They stood back up and took cover behind a shoulder-height wall. They then ran singly to the next closest hiding spot. Heading toward the shootout.

The referee left a trail of blood behind him.

81 The first shot—not the one that had gone out but the one that came in—finished demolishing the already damaged window. The next shot landed somewhere, but Thembinkosi didn't spend long wondering where.

He had fallen back a few steps when High Voice had aimed at him. By the time the first two shots had been launched outside, he was already in the process of falling to the floor. His head landed against the wardrobe wall as Thembinkosi tried in vain to catch himself somehow with his hands. The blow hurt, a lot. But what shocked him even more than his own pain was Nozipho's scream. She must have thought he'd been hit.

Timing. Thembinkosi fell deeper into the wardrobe. Now a barrage of bullets hailed in from the outside. Deep Voice leaped to the side to escape them. As he did that, he pulled a giant gun out from somewhere. And he glanced over at Thembinkosi—if I didn't have other things to do, I'd shoot you. When Thembinkosi landed with his upper body in the wardrobe, he called: "Stay in there! Get down!"

Getting down was what the two others were doing even though his words weren't meant for them. Shots flew into the room, and the two men didn't risk moving out of their defensive positions. The response to the one shot fired by High Voice had been too massive. Thembinkosi pulled up his legs and tried to draw his entire body into the protection of the wardrobe. As he was about to pull the door shut behind him, a salvo of gunfire shredded the upper part of the door.

"Stop!" a loud voice shouted from outside.

He didn't know if that was meant for the two whites hidden in the room or for the people out on the street shooting into the house. The shots slowly petered out. One last one struck a bedroom wall, but then everything was quiet.

82 Moses watched the bleeding referee and the two guards. The fat man who had struggled to climb over the wall was having a hard time following the other two. The second guard took the lead, followed by the referee, who was holding his head with one hand and stretching one hand out in front of him to keep his balance. After taking cover behind a car parked outside a garage, they checked their surroundings and waited on number three.

On the one hand, this is good, Moses thought. The attention was no longer focused on him. Someone had done something else, so hunting him down was no longer as urgent as it had been. Retreat. Take the furthest route to the exit along the wall. Try to escape. On the other hand...

It might be good to know what was going on over there. Maybe it would be helpful for him to know what was so important. Helpful for his escape.

The shots died down.

Moses looked around. In the distance, the mail carrier was standing and chatting with somebody who was hidden by a tree. Impossible to tell who that might be. A Polo drove up beside the two of them, came to a stop. A window was lowered, brief exchange. The Polo drove on and stopped in front of a house. Nothing in sight the other way.

Moses ran across the street and down the one the other three had already taken. They had a major head start on him. He took the first opportunity to hide behind a large, mid-height bush.

There was one thing he needed to avoid at all costs: The

other three shouldn't see that he was following them.

 It wasn't really quiet. At least, not for long. Not even a little.

People were yelling. The dog was barking again. More than one police siren was going off in the distance. Thembinkosi listened to the nearby breathing of the two whites, which sounded as loud as a power plant. Behind him, Nozipho was sobbing. A weeping full of fear and desolation.

That was good. As long as she was crying, she was alive.

Thembinkosi's vision was blocked by the half-shredded wardrobe door. He couldn't see out the window. He was lying half in, half out of the wardrobe, his arms crooked over his head. High Voice was stretched out on his stomach between the bed and the window. He didn't see any blood. He could see Deep Voice's head, also on the floor, turned away from him. Neither of them was moving.

"We're going in," a male voice outside declared.

"Absolutely not!" Another male voice.

The dog barked.

"Carl?" High Voice said quietly. "Carl?"

"Hm?"

"You okay?"

"Uh-huh."

Thembinkosi didn't know if that was good news or bad. Neither of them had moved a millimeter, but they were alive. What did that mean?

If they were dead, the people outside wouldn't need to keep shooting, he thought.

Except at him and Nozipho. Would they first ask who they were and what they were doing in the house? Not likely.

He slowly reached a hand to the wall that separated the wardrobe partitions. He scratched a fingernail down it. An answering scratch quickly came from the other side.

"Carl?"

"Hm?"

"What should we do?"

"Survive."

"Exactly! That's what I was thinking."

High Voice's body tensed. He was stretched out like a swastika on the floor. One hand holding his pistol, the other not. The hand not holding the pistol pushed off a little from the floor. A silent wave gradually moved through his entire body. One knee reacted with similar pressure, and High Voice was already halfway to the shot-out window.

"What are you doing?" Deep Voice asked. He began to crawl after the other man.

"Surviving!" With this word, he lifted his pistol over the edge of the windowsill and began to shoot.

"No!" Deep Voice shouted.

The first reaction from those outside was a man yelling, "Get down!"

84 The two guards and the referee reached a cross street, and hastily disappeared around the corner. Whatever had just happened over there, the three of them weren't all that far away from it. Moses imagined how the street under his feet curved slightly as it moved forward. The shooting had to be happening along there. In any case, it had just stopped. Maybe everything was already over.

He had to be careful. Two more properties on both sides, and then he would also reach the cross street. He glanced around. The coast was clear. Nobody at the intersection. Another look over the houses he wanted to pass. Nothing.

Stop. He looked back one more time and saw a woman standing at the edge of a window. She had straight, blonde hair and was wearing large glasses. Older than him, though not by much. Standing stock still. Staring at him. He greeted her with a nod and then ran to the next wall.

One more yard, and he'd be able to see down the next intersection.

Now. Moses sprinted as fast as he could. As fast as he

still could after all the previous running. The shooting started up again as he made a beeline for the next wall, dove across, and crouched down on the other side. He had no idea how far away the bullets were flying, but he was close enough to feel panicked.

Calmly inhale. Exhale. In. Out. Stay down for just a few more seconds, then take the next step. The gunfire broke off again. This didn't make him feel any better, though.

"Hey!" a voice called, one he knew all too well.

Shit, he thought and automatically rolled himself up tighter, one eye peeking over the top of the wall.

A figure came running up to the intersection, looked around and took off again, almost stumbling. Moses couldn't believe it. The man looked like him. Okay, somewhat older. He was almost the same height, but the jeans he was wearing were the same shade as his. His yellow t-shirt was a few degrees darker, but was also tight-fitting. His hair wasn't quite as bushy as his, but was still a typical afro. Moses saw the man running his way and had the feeling that he was looking into a mirror.

Behind him was the jackass from earlier. His nemesis. Club in the one hand, something else in the other. He was drawing closer.

"Hey!" he hollered again. And: "Stop, you bastard!"

Then, he himself stopped. And Moses could now see exactly what he had in his other hand. He threw his club aside and steadied the object in both hands. Aimed.

One second ticked by before he fired a shot.

The other man was almost up to his location. Moses saw him lurch, then fall. Less than two meters separated the man and himself. The white man's steps came closer.

Moses flattened himself as much as possible against the wall. Be invisible. Don't even breathe.

And then somewhere else, the great shootout began again.

Keep breathing.

The second reaction was a shot that penetrated the wardrobe door. Splinters rained down on Thembinkosi, and he tried to make himself even smaller.

The third reaction was massive gunfire. Everything blazing all at once. It was as if what had happened a moment before had just been a foretaste of what was coming. Hundreds of shooters were firing into the room. Make that thousands. The entire army and the police and all the security guards in the world, all together. Thembinkosi shut his eyes and thought about praying. But it didn't work. He'd never learned how. Instead he scratched the wood behind him. Tears sprang to his eyes when he felt the response from the other side.

The maelstrom was heavy, but it didn't last long. It broke off at some point, and he risked opening his eyes to look to the side. High Voice was lying on his back, bleeding. He'd been hit everywhere—head, torso, legs. Deep Voice was still concealed by the bed. Only his feet were visible. However, a pool of blood was gradually collecting on the floor beside him.

A shout from outside. "Slowly!" And: "Be careful!"

Thembinkosi was also being careful. Just don't move.

"All clear?"

"Yes."

"What?"

"Nothing."

"Closer."

"Yes, sir." Two voices.

"Careful!"

"Yes, sir." The same two voices.

The conversation was coming closer. Thembinkosi thought he could hear footsteps on the lawn. He had to swallow. Had a very bad feeling.

"Everything's fine," a voice spoke into the room. Couldn't have meant the room itself.

"Are you sure?"

"Yes."

"Secure it."

"Okay."

Thembinkosi imagined himself growing smaller and smaller until he disappeared.

Metallic noises from outside. Click and clack. One safety, then another. Then it started. Thembinkosi didn't close his eyes this time. The shots destroyed what still remained of the two men. The bed as well, the mattress. The shots buried themselves into the wardrobe, the walls, surely the hallway also. Something outside the room shattered. *Devastation,* Thembinkosi thought. *Don't just break, completely annihilate.* A bullet landed right next to him, then another above him. He thought about Nozipho and how much he loved her.

Then it stopped.

"Everything's secure?" From a distance outside the house.

"Completely secure." From closer.

 Moses waited. And thought about the blonde woman. She'd seen everything, too.

The white man had...Moses was shaking. The white man had shot him, Moses. That had been his intention.

He had to know what had happened. He slowly lifted his head. Used his arms. Peered over the short wall.

The other man was lying there. Moses looked at him and began to tremble even more. That was him lying there.

Maybe he was still alive. Moses shifted his gaze. The woman was gone. Maybe she was calling the police.

No, the police were already here. She didn't need to call anyone. The white man was also gone.

The great shootout finally stopped again.

Moses stood up. Looked around one more time. He sprinted the few steps over to the man. Leaned down. Turned him over. Damp crotch. He was dead.

Turned him back over. Caught sight of the hole in the

back of his head. The bullet had lodged itself there.

Moses began to cry. Who was this guy? Someone... some man...wrong place, wrong time...some black man, he thought, too. Some black man. He now caught sight of his shoes. Converse knockoffs, years of wear, tattered. The hole at the shoulder of his shirt. The rip in the seat of his jeans.

Some poor black man. Moses straightened up. He would avenge him.

 "Completely secure."

That's what the voice had said.

Thembinkosi scratched on the wardrobe wall. At the same moment, Nozipho did the same from her side.

"Did anyone hear the other shot?" Outside.

"Shot?" A different voice.

"I did." Another voice.

"No." Numerous voices.

"Something happened."

"Car backfire."

"A shot. Unmistakable."

How could a single shot be so important? he wondered. *What could have possibly happened to make all this less important?* Thembinkosi looked around. The attention outside was no longer focused on the room. He moved his head. Outside, footsteps moving away from them. Asphalt. High Voice was completely mangled. His clothes were barely recognizable. His head was a pulp, his arms which he had used to shield himself no longer had any attached muscles. All his blood had leaked out. *And to think the media was locked in a debate about whether the South African police took their work seriously*, he marveled.

"Yes, a shot."

"But where?"

"Really?"

"Couldn't have been a shot. Not on your life."

"From over there."

"...go over..."

Deep Voice hadn't fared any better. His feet were gone, and his blood was now mingling with High Voice's. Thembinkosi looked away.

The voices outside were fading away.

"Go search the house!" a male voice ordered.

"Yes, sir!" came the answer.

Thembinkosi again heard Nozipho's scratching behind him.

 Moses looked around one more time. No faces in the windows. Good Lord, someone had just been shot out here. And not all that far off, there'd just been... just been...a massacre. The people should all be staring out their windows. Were they hiding? Or were they really all still at work?

From somewhere, he heard footsteps approach. He also heard a car. No, make that two. He quickly jumped back behind the wall he'd been using. Flipped around as he crouched down. One eye above the top of the wall. Just in time.

An entire army came around the corner. First the cops on foot with a dog, two police cars, followed by a couple of security vehicles. A bakkie, too. *Don't think about it,* Moses told himself. Don't think about the chap who'd tried to run him over earlier. Then two Polos. Behind the security cars came the guards. Two of them in civilian clothing.

Too many for Moses. Many too many. If he was lucky, he might manage to slip away. He turned onto his stomach and crawled along the wall until he reached the shadow of the house.

"We got him," someone cried.

Moses gave a start, but then realized that they meant the other man. The dead man.

More crawling, dragging himself through a dry bed. Holding back a cough. More voices behind him. Chaos.

"Finally."

"But who was that in the house?"

"...escaped..."

"...won't rob anyone else..."

"...ran away..."

"...didn't have to end like this..."

"...a job here..."

"...the police..."

"...their responsibility..."

"...heard a shot..."

"But who shot him?" a woman's voice asked.

Everyone fell silent. The dog barked.

Moses turned back, knelt down beside an ornamental bush, and watched the scene. The people in the cars had now gotten out. They were all gathered in a circle around the body. Nobody said anything. A police siren briefly chirped somewhere in the distance. The people in the circle studied each other. It wasn't clear if they were searching for a hero or someone to blame.

One of them turned around. Then another. Slowly, the whole group turned to face the direction from which the dead man had just come.

Moses could see their bodies tense up. Still no one was saying a word.

And right on the edge of his line of vision, Moses saw the white man come to a stop. Club in the one hand. The other hand empty.

He stopped, legs spread. Began to hit the club into his other palm.

"I took care of the kaffir," he cried.

 89 Thembinkosi raised his head and looked through the splintered door. Where the window had been... All that remained were a few remnants of the wooden frame. He carefully stood up. Nobody outside was looking into the room. Instead, he heard people moving around the front door.

"We have to get out of here." Nozipho was looking out of her half of the wardrobe. "They'll do the same thing to us."

"Yes. But where?"

Someone was slamming into the front door. They heard a cracking sound. They didn't have much time to figure out a solution. Nozipho's voice was right against his ear. "I know where..."

"Where?"

"There's only one place!"

"No!" Thembinkosi cried. "No!"

"Yes. Take your shoes off."

"Why?"

Crash. The front door was starting to give way.

"Let me try," a voice outside insisted.

"Do it. Take them off."

Nozipho was already holding her shoes and standing in her socks in High Voice's blood. She stepped over him and onto the bed where she began to put her sneakers back on.

Thembinkosi loosened the ties on his leather shoes, yanked them off, and copied Nozipho's movements. On the bed, he stuck his blood-soaked stockinged feet back into his shoes.

"Jump!" Nozipho said.

When he hesitated, she gave him a little push.

The door was splintering under someone's shoulder.

Thembinkosi leaped over Deep Voice and landed in the hallway. His feet made a squishing sound in his shoes.

"One more time," came from outside.

Nozipho spread the bullet-tattered bedspread out so their bloody footprints were out of sight, then she also jumped.

"Go!" she urged as she wiped away a drop of blood that had spurted out from Thembinkosi's shoe. "Go!" She now shoved him hard.

The front door broke apart. Someone tumbled into the lounge. Nozipho quietly opened the door to the garage, pushing Thembinkosi inside. She shut the door and hurried over to the freezer. She held the lid up and waited.

When Thembinkosi didn't react immediately, she said: "We don't have a choice."

"And don't even think that you'll be lying on top of me," she added a second later.

90

2:53:17

"I took care of the kaffir," the white man yelled.

Legs spread, smug, a trace of a grin on his ugly face. Jay-Jay Dlomo held Nkosi tightly against him and said nothing. Nobody in the circle made a sound. But the dog wanted something. Dlomo could sense it. Nkosi couldn't speak, but made up for that in his ability to run and jump and bite. Jay-Jay knew this dog and adored him. He had molded him into his own image as much as you can do that with an animal. And Dlomo was completely certain the dog was feeling what he was feeling right now. Loathing. Loathing toward the white idiot. How arrogant he was. How he stood there waiting for something to happen. Dlomo slowly leaned down. He caressed Nkosi's head and murmured: "Go ahead."

The dog trembled and strained against his leash. With his thumb and forefinger, Dlomo pinched the ring on the harness. Nkosi's tugging was rewarded. He didn't even need to pull to verify his freedom. He availed himself of it instantaneously. One, two, three, four leaps and he was within striking distance of the white man. Everyone's eyes were on the dog. Only the white man was watching Dlomo. And Dlomo was gazing into his eyes. Hopefully, he'd had time to realize how closely triumph and defeat were linked. Nkosi was airborne. His legs were extended into the spring, his jaws wide. In anticipation of warm flesh. White flesh. *Do it, Nkosi*, Dlomo thought.

2:53:25

Stevie van Lange had just reached The Pines as the shooting started. Ugly affair. It was the company's responsibility to prevent things like this from getting out of hand and blood being spilled. And God knew blood was flowing. Now that jerk was standing here. A loser in the new system. Not every white had been able to maintain their previous standard of living. Of course. Regardless, no one needed to talk like this. Sometimes it was necessary to kill someone—this was a violent country, after all. But not because of skin color. Skin color was no longer a factor. But nobody was arguing against what the jerk had said. The dog handler leaned down slightly. A low growl from the dog. Like a warning. Stevie automatically reached behind his back and under his shirt. The animal only needed a few strides to launch himself. Stevie was already cocking his pistol. A stabilizing step backward with his right foot. Focus. Track the dog with both arms. Fire. By the time the dog reached the white man, all of his energy had already drained away. He took the man down and then remained on top of him.

2:53:37

White people had lost their freaking minds. Yolanda Baker wanted to blast the jerk's head off of his shoulders. Reached for her holster, while nobody said a word.

The way he was standing there. But then the dog startled her. She momentarily loosened her grip on her gun. A good practice she'd spent long enough drilling. Grab your gun, release your gun, grab your gun again. The dog was already in the air when she noticed the other white man was aiming his gun at her. She pulled out her service pistol as swiftly as she could and cocked it. Registered that the young white man wasn't aiming at her at all. He was tracking the dog. But she had already shifted gears. Yolanda Baker could no longer stop the motion sequence she had trained for so often. In the miniscule acoustic interval between the white man's shot and her own, she thought: *Just stop, pull your weapon up.* But she couldn't manage that in time. She shot the man in the chest. The fountain of blood out of it was the last thing she saw.

2:53:41

People didn't say kaffir anymore. It didn't fit the times, Gerrit van Lange was thinking when the dog started its attack. The group's mood instantly changed. From the baffled astonishment that had descended when the idiot had appeared to this tension that didn't bode well for a leaderless unit. Too late, he caught sight of his son, in his own state of tension, trying to compensate for that state by reaching behind his back. He was still so young. *Don't do it,* Gerrit van Lange thought. His eyes flitted across the part of the group he could see without turning his head. The young policewoman was watching Stevie, as she pulled her pistol out of her holster with shaking hands. Van Lange tried to comprehend what both movements meant, but the distance between them was too great. He registered the dog, which was now strangely airborne. Floating. A frozen image. He saw Stevie only as a particle, his movement, his step backward, because he couldn't take his eyes off the police officer. Whose weapon was pointed at his son. Gerrit van Lange shoved his right hand under his flowing shirt as he sprang forward. Two people were between him and the officer. As he fell, he twisted around as he'd been taught in the army. The fall seriously hurt his shoulder, but by the time he hit the pavement, he had already squeezed off his shot.

2:53:19

The pig. They should shoot him in his tracks. From behind his ornamental bush, Moses watched the group of people caught in lethargy. Why weren't they doing anything? He had murdered a person. The white man had slaughtered him. Him, Moses. Why wasn't anyone furious? Why were they just standing there? The only one moving was the man with the dog that was blocked from his line of sight. He was doing something with the animal. That was the second it dashed off. Moses saw its front and back paws push off the pavement, again and then again. One last time and the dog was leaping at his target. Something was happening after all. At least, he had understood that much. The white man still hadn't grasped that, hadn't even raised his hands to fend off the teeth that were a second away from ripping his skin. *A millisecond and vengeance would be achieved*, Moses thought. He didn't hear the shot until his eyes saw its devastation. Just like your senses can betray you if everything falls apart in your life. The dog continued to fly through the air toward the white man, slamming into him like the fist of a powerful boxer. Moses then heard the shot, and then another, and then another. And as these first shots catalyzed what followed, he threw himself back down on his stomach.

 "She still isn't completely cold," Nozipho said.
"I know."

Nozipho was lying on top of Thembinkosi, stomach to stomach. She had wrapped her bare arms around him, shoulders pressed against the freezer wall.

"She also isn't completely dry," Thembinkosi said.
"Yuck. And it's so cold in here."
"It was too hot a moment ago. You saved us."
The garage door opened.
"Psst," Nozipho hissed into Thembinkosi's ear.
"Garage."
"Freezer."
"Leave it."
"We're supposed to check everywhere."
"Don't overdo it. Come on."
The door again. Both of them exhaled.
"You saved us," Thembinkosi repeated.
"We're not out yet. Where's the briefcase?"
"In the wardrobe."
"Shit."
"And your purse?"
"Also in the wardrobe."
"They'll find them."
"Nonsense. They're looking for people, not bags. They

won't even touch them."

"But how can we get out of here now?"

"The back door."

"In the kitchen?"

"Uh-huh. Simple lock."

"But they're still in the house, aren't they?"

"No idea. I'm so cold."

 "I'll be right there," Warren Kramer had said as he left the control room.

Happiness had been working at Meyer Investment for only a few months, but she was already well-versed in her supervisor's language. The boss had to go somewhere. Translated as: See, I have everything under control.

That was fine with her. She now had one less gated community to supervise. She was in the process of following a couple of young men in overalls in Paradise on Sea in Nahoon. They were on foot in the newest subdivision in her monitor group. Some of the houses there had views of the ocean, others were located on the golf course. One of the two men was carrying a ladder over his shoulder, and both of them were carrying empty backpacks. There was no white boss anywhere in sight who was telling them what to do. It was quite late to start a new job. The digital clock on the monitors read 2:52. Where were the two of them heading? A ladder could mean roof work, tree cutting, or burglary. She was now switching between the cameras in Paradise on Sea to try to find them again.

There they were. Three o'clock in the afternoon. That was definitely too late to start a job. She was now certain that the two men were wandering around all on their own. What should she do?

Call Warren? He was in The Pines, and it was a real mess over there. Old van Lange and his son were both there already, so maybe she should call someone at Central Alert. Or the police.

She was picking up the receiver from the desk phone when her eyes fell on the monitor on which the words "The Pines" had been written in marker. A large group of people had gathered near an intersection, and they were waiting on something. Central Alert, the police, others. She recognized the two van Langes. The camera was shooting the group from the side, and straight down the road on which it was trained stood that guy Warren Kramer was always griping about. What would he say if he saw him now?

Right: recreational security. The white man was standing a bit apart from the group, and somehow she had the feeling that all the others were watching him.

Happiness typed in the code that gave this camera priority status. She had to look closely to verify that the video stream hadn't crashed. Nobody in the group seemed to be moving. She now noticed one of the cops leaning down slightly. She couldn't tell what he was doing, because he was partially blocked by some of the others. Then a collective shiver seemed to go through the group, and something shot out of it.

It took Happiness a moment to realize that the thing was a dog. He was sprinting toward the white man Kramer was always making fun of. The dog then launched himself at the man as everything happened simultaneously. The young van Lange, who was standing closer to the white guy than most of the others, was suddenly holding something in his hand. A little flash of lightning shot out of the end of it. The dog then collided with the white guy. The young van Lange crumpled, as the dog took down the white guy. She recognized old van Lange as he dove onto the pavement. A female cop also collapsed. Another police officer bent over van Lange, and the Central Alert boss convulsed a few times.

The phone fell from her hand.

At the same time, the monitor for Paradise on the Sea was showing the two men in overalls climbing out of a second-floor window. Their backpacks were practically exploding.

Yolanda Baker's head was destroyed before she hit the ground. The projectile from Gerrit van Lange's pistol had made a couple of rounds through her skull.

Two seconds before her back struck the curb, Warrant Officer Vukile Pokwana took a step forward and emptied his clip into the body of Gerrit van Lange. He did this without much thought. It was more reflex than considered plan. If one of his officers was attacked, there was only one response for him: to neutralize the source of danger. As he stood over van Lange, whom he had known for years, he sensed how absurd everything seemed in this situation in which they had stumbled. He sank one more bullet into the body and caught sight of the racist standing up and running away. He was about to aim his pistol at the fleeing man to shoot him in the back when he had the feeling that hot and cold water were both surging through his body, at war with one another. For some reason, he recognized the tingling that came along with this. However, he wasn't in any position to actually formulate any thoughts about it. He toppled onto the Central Alert boss without even an attempt to catch himself, smashing his forehead against the street's asphalt.

Bismarck van Vuuren leaped over the closest wall and rolled away. That hurt, but he was sure this was less painful than a bullet between the ribs. In his flight, he'd abandoned the taser he'd just fired, simply dropped it. Hitting the grass, he flipped over and saw Warren Kramer and a white cop land next to him. They glanced at each other briefly. This reminded him of his military service in Angola—that had been a long time ago. On the other side of the street, the Central Alert bodybuilder and two of his coworkers reached safety. A black cop followed by the dog handler ran in the same direction and dove to the ground. Rob van der Merwe hit the grass next to him. Where had he come from?

94 "Should we try?" Nozipho asked. Her bare upper arms were pressed against the walls of the freezer. "I'm freezing."

"Do you hear anything?"

"Not a sound. But I'm also just cold. And I have to pee so badly."

"Me, too... Do you think we should give it a shot?"

Nozipho didn't bother to answer, but pushed the lid up with her ass. The oppressive heat mixed with the chill, and Nozipho got goosebumps. She lifted the lid with one arm and listened for sounds inside the house.

"Empty?" Thembinkosi asked.

"I think so."

A shot was fired somewhere. Then another. A third. Then a barrage.

"That's nowhere close," Thembinkosi said.

Nozipho tugged her dress up over her hips and climbed out of the freezer. She then pulled the fabric back down. Thembinkosi was already standing next to her. Very quietly, she opened the door to the house, just a crack.

The real battle was now underway. Shots fired from various guns. Irregular. They looked at each other. Nozipho preceded Thembinkosi into the house. She walked straight into the bathroom and sat on the toilet. Thembinkosi followed her and peed into the sink.

"Unlock the back door," she told Thembinkosi.

She then waded through the blood to the wardrobe and fetched the briefcase and purse. By the time she reached the kitchen, the back door was already open. The shooting had stopped.

 95 Mouth wide, Happiness was staring at the monitor. The phone rang down on the floor, but she didn't react.

The guy who'd been knocked down by the dog rolled

out from underneath the animal and ran away. Both of her bosses were lying on the ground. As well as the female police officer. And the black male cop, too. The other people were scrambling for safety. The shooting resumed. She would have given anything for sound footage.

This had been a single group a moment ago, she thought. Now it was everyone for themselves, looking and turning and making decisions. Either the one side or the other.

She now caught sight of Hlaudi, who was gazing in one direction. He took a step that way before glancing across and deciding on that option. He flopped onto the ground more than he actually fell. *So many muscles*, Happiness recalled. *But such a small cock. Sad.*

The street was now empty. Except for the corpses. The others were concealed behind walls on both sides of the road. Were they shooting again? Happiness stared hard at the monitor, but she couldn't tell.

96 Moses had flattened himself against the ground as much as possible. Screams from people trying to reach safety. With one cheek pressed against the dirt, he could watch the street with one eye. He saw people who were in the same situation as he was. Searching for cover, lying on the ground. Nobody was shooting at this point.

Who had actually fired their guns? More yelling.

"...started..."

"...murder..."

Much he couldn't understand. Panic-stricken people. A few were lying on the street. Dead or injured.

And who had been the target?

He saw the bare legs of the referee. A police officer. A civilian. Another cop. And someone who looked like a work-man in tattered jeans but expensive shoes. Something was off in the image in front of him. However, before he could figure out what it was, someone across the street started shooting again.

His side of the street fired back immediately. He had to get out of here as quickly as possible. Moses pivoted in the dirt and crept off.

97 Hlaudi landed chest-first on a cop's leg when he hit the ground on the other side of the waist-high wall. The policeman screamed and kicked at him with his other leg. Another cop lying next to the one he'd just landed on stretched out an arm. Hlaudi wanted to call out something like "No!" or "Don't!" but the shot had already been fired. A bullet was immediately shot back. The cop who had fired first collapsed dead. The officer right next to him pulled his gun out of its holster and hurled himself at the wall. Hlaudi knocked him off his feet, but he had already been hit by a bullet. They were taking non-stop fire from across the street. The man had been struck in the shoulder, and he was cradling his arm in pain.

"Give me that!" Hlaudi ordered him.

The intensity of the gunfire from the other side now abated. He glanced around quickly and saw Ludelwa lying on the ground, too. His coworker had her hand pressed to a wound in her throat, and she was bleeding profusely. She didn't seem to be moving, either.

The wall on the other side of the street was only half as high as the one behind which they'd been able to take cover. Despite that, they were still putting up a good fight. The man who had brought the dog materialized beside him. He was also holding a gun. They nodded at each other and lifted themselves far enough over the wall to shoot. Hlaudi counted off their shots. One from him, one from dog man, one from him—a hit, one from dog man—another hit. They looked at each other and almost simultaneously fell backward.

"We got three of them."

"How many are left?" dog man asked.

"Two or three."

"Wait or keep going?"

"We outnumber them. If a couple of us can draw fire from here, we could take them from behind."

Hlaudi held the dead cop's hand above the wall. It was immediately hit by a bullet. Hlaudi dropped the arm. He and dog man started off. Back behind the house here, then on to the next one, away from the exit to the gated community. On to the next house and then over to the street. Look around, across, behind the closest house, then count backward. One, two, three. They were now behind the others.

They had to be careful not to become victims of friendly fire. Dog man pointed at his chest, then down the side of the house. They were standing behind the house in front of which the whites had taken up their positions. Hlaudi nodded and indicated to the other man that he was going to go down the other side of the house.

That was it in terms of discussion between dog man and him. Be cautious, see what was going on at the wall, shoot. The people on this side wouldn't be waiting for them. They had enough to do simply trying to survive.

He crouched down behind a bush with colorful flowers. Both sides were firing. As he leaned against the wall of the house, he could feel the bullet strikes. He slowly extended his head forward and saw five men. All stretched out on the ground. Two of them had obvious head wounds, another was wounded, possibly dead. Two were still firing. Hlaudi pulled his head back. Concentrated. When he stuck it back out again, he wanted to take a shot. Hand extended, head behind it. There were now fewer shots being fired. Reloading. Empty clips.

He could now see that three of them were dead. Nonverbal communication between the two survivors. He couldn't make out about what. He aimed at the blonde man in the polo shirt.

Fired.

In the back of his head.

The man in shorts turned around and took two bullets

instantly. One of his and one of dog man's. Slumped to the side.

"Cease fire!" dog man called. "Cease fire!"

Wait. No sound. Hlaudi peered around the house corner and saw dog man doing the same thing. Both of them flashed a thumb's up. All clear. They moved to the front of the house.

They didn't notice that the man in shorts was still moving a little. He raised his pistol and fired at dog man's heart.

Dog man collapsed. Hlaudi spun around at the same moment and fired two more rounds into the man on the ground. With that, his police pistol was empty.

 "You have blood on your shoes," Thembinkosi pointed out as he took the briefcase from Nozipho.

"That's okay," she said. "It'll come off. Let's get out of here. Where are the shots coming from?"

"Over there," Thembinkosi said. "We need to go in the other direction, anyway."

"We look like shit."

"We can't do anything about it. I feel better than I did in the wardrobe or the freezer. Even if my suit's going to be stained after this. Come on..." He wiped his forehead with his suit sleeve.

They slipped around the next house and froze when they reached the street. Looked both ways.

Nozipho straightened Thembinkosi's jacket. "Let's first head over to the outer wall." She pointed across the street at the next row of houses. "I'd feel better over there. The further I am from that house, the better I'll feel. And then we can follow the wall. To the exit."

 Moses stopped at the next cross street. Knocked the dirt off his pants and t-shirt. Behind him, the gunfire sounded like a full-blown war. Had all this happened because of him? *Couldn't be*, he thought.

The house across the street looked empty. He ran to the other side of the street and stopped once he'd passed it. Checked out the next house and sprinted to the next street. The house in front of him wasn't empty. He saw a woman in the lounge, but her back was turned toward him. *Didn't matter anymore*, he thought. He had to keep going. He had to get out. To the wall, then on to the exit. And then... Something had to work out.

Past the house. To the outer wall. Had he already been here today? Definitely. He had been everywhere already. He briefly crouched down and tried to see down the long stretch between the wall and the houses. All the way to the end. Then to the right, and somewhere past that point the exit had to be located. The view in both directions was free and clear. Of course, people could be concealed behind the walls, hedges, and bushes.

He would have to solve that problem if it arose.

Moses set off. Jumped over a hedge. Then over a wall. Then over another one that was high. Could feel how heavy his legs were by now.

Be careful, he warned himself. The wall he was approaching was fairly tall again, and he jumped with all the strength that remained in him. Was already focusing on the next obstacle.

He had hardly landed before he took off again. The blow was so powerful that it knocked all the air out of him. No feeling inside, no thought. End of existence. No god was strong enough to withstand an assault like this. Right into his stomach.

His supporting leg had just been searching for and had found the ground. The other was still in the air and had wanted to carry his body a few meters more. The counter-force drove him back in the direction he'd just come. For an eternity, Moses hung in the air, almost weightless, but then he crumpled to the ground.

"Pig!" someone yelled.

Shit! thought Moses as blood once again surged through his brain.

It was him again. And now he finally had the better cards. The club was already rushing down at him. Moses wanted to vomit.

 "Come again?" the female voice from Central said. "What do you mean they're all dead?"

"I mean that they're all dead."

"Slowly. Are you Warrant Officer Mafu?"

"Yes."

"The break-in at the gated community."

"The whites started it."

"What?" the woman asked.

"They shot first."

"Officer...Are you really Warrant Officer Mafu?"

"It's the whites' fault."

"But who are the whites?"

"The whites...are the whites!"

"And now everyone's dead."

"Yes."

"Who's dead?"

"Bezuidenhout."

"The Warrant Officer?"

"Yes."

"He's white."

"Dead."

"Who else?"

"Baker. Constable Baker."

"Dead?"

"Dead."

"Who killed her?"

"The whites."

"But Bezuidenhout is also white."

"Yes."

"And who killed him?"

"The dog handler."

"Inspector Dlomo?"

"Yes."

"And where is he?"

"Dead."

"And who killed him?"

"The whites."

 "Police," Nozipho said. "It's the police." She pointed down the wall at a group of people.

"Shit!" Thembinkosi said. "We need to disappear in the other direction."

"They've already seen us."

A young woman in uniform waved at them. "Over here."

They slowly turned toward the officer behind whom the others were gathered.

"Okay. Better than being shot to pieces in the wardrobe," Thembinkosi said.

"We weren't shot to pieces."

"We almost were."

"Now we'll just do what we'd planned all along."

"Didn't you get a phone call?" the officer asked once they reached her.

In a cul de sac that ended at the wall, several garbage collectors were standing around, their large truck parked a short distance behind them. As well as a mail carrier, a heavyset woman in a green smock, two boys in overalls, and a couple of people in civilian clothing. The stench of rotting garbage stood over the scene like a tent.

"Must've missed it," Thembinkosi said. "Why?"

"This entire area back there is under lockdown. We're searching for a tsotsi," she said. "A dangerous tsotsi."

"We heard the shooting." Nozipho.

"Wild." Thembinkosi.

"Yes, everyone's heard about it." The officer.

"Did you win?" Thembinkosi.

"Don't they always?" Nozipho tugged at her dress and tried to smile at the officer. She was hiding the tear in the fabric with her purse.

"I think so." The officer. "But I haven't heard anything. You'll need to wait here for a while, until I get further orders."

 "You pig!" the white man shrieked as he punched him.

Moses tried to protect himself. But the guy was kneeling on one of his arms, so he only had one available to fend off the blows. An open hand now slapped him across the face. That hurt.

He's not heavy or all that strong, Moses thought. But he had taken Moses by surprise and overcome him. *Just go slack,* he told himself, *just for a second.*

The other man noticed the relaxation and interpreted it as capitulation. He started to grin, and slapped him once more, hard. Moses then tightened his muscles and jerked his knee up between the white man's legs, who instantaneously shriveled up like a spider. *Bullseye,* Moses thought. He pushed the guy off and tried to stand up. But the other man had clenched his fingers around his t-shirt. He still wouldn't let go, even when the fabric began to tear.

Moses made a fist and punched the man in the head. The blow seemed to have an effect. The man rolled a little further to the side. The t-shirt continued to rip. Moses pried the man's fingers apart and stood up. A knockout. The other man wasn't moving anymore. Moses caught sight of a cigarette packet in his shirt pocket, and he pulled it out.

As he was about to dash off, he recalled the pistol. There was no way he was going to get shot in the back like his double. Leaned down, rolled the white man on his other side, patted him down. The gun was stuck into the back of his pants.

He pulled his arm back to throw it over the wall, but then he paused. If they found it with his fingerprints on it, things could take a horrible turn. *That...* he thought... *would be worse than all the nightmare things that had already happened today.* He stuffed the thing into his own pants. He then looked at the cigarettes in his other hand and thought: *One drag, just one drag.*

He kicked the white man in the side. Then once more.

103 The four garbage workers were standing in a group, talking. The mail carrier was hanging around close to them. Maybe they had just been chatting. The rest were gathered in a separate, silent group. They were studying the newcomers. The officer was standing off by herself, her head cocked to the side as if she wanted to talk into the mic dangling off her collar.

Nozipho walked up to the trash workers. Thembinkosi could tell how uncomfortable she felt in her torn dress. It had some stains by this point, too. She was still pressing the purse against her side to cover the tear.

"Hi," she said.

The garbage workers still seemed a little watchful, distrustful. They saw an attractive woman from a class to which they could never belong, not the grime on her dress.

"Hi," she repeated. "What's actually going on here?" All four of them started talking at once.

"...tsotsi...shameless...break-in...young guy...rape jewelry and cash...whole army..." Etcetera.

The workers shared what they knew. And it was evident that they respected the boy. They all knew someone who made a living from not-quite-legal activities. And they had all heard the shootout. The boy was dead, and he had died a hero's death. The newspapers would publish something about him tomorrow. Thembinkosi hoped he'd never be in the newspaper. What a nightmare!

Nozipho came right back. "Funny," she said.

"Yes, what a coincidence."

"Which coincidence?"

"That with the boy," Thembinkosi's voice grew very quiet. "I saw him running. Had to happen at some point—competition that would be on the move the same time we were. And in such a large gated community like this one!"

"Nonsense." Nozipho's voice was barely audible. She pressed close against Thembinkosi.

"What do you mean, nonsense?"

"Didn't you hear? The jewelry? That was us."

"Us?"

"Us. They were hunting the boy because of us."

"And the rape?"

"No idea. But they'll soon see that he doesn't have the jewelry. Then they'll wonder where it could be. We have to get out."

"Of course, we have to get out."

"Thembi, not just whenever. Now!"

 Moses extracted the matchbook and then a cigarette from the packet. One drag. Chesterfield wasn't his favorite, but that didn't matter. The one drag would help. He looked down at the white man who hadn't moved. He felt like kicking him in the face.

Cigarette between his lips. Tear off a match. Slowly scrape it across the stripe. Watch the flame ignite. Hold up to the cigarette. Inhale. Into his lungs.

Whoa!

Hold his breath. Another second, then another. Savor it. He loved the initial feeling of dizziness that descended when you hadn't lit up in a while.

The flame had reached his fingers. Moses began to cough and dropped the match. One more cough. He had to keep going. He also dropped the cigarette, stepped on it, and set off.

He still had a long way to go.

He started to run. Gained speed and felt a need to take one last look at the crazy white man. Not that there was any way he could be following him. Stopped. Turned back.

The white man actually was struggling to climb over a wall, sluggishly but determinedly.

And where he had dropped the match and the cigarette, the dry lawn had started to smolder. Moses saw the smoke and the disconcerting flicker of a small flame.

 Nozipho pulled Thembinkosi's arm. "Come on, let's go."

"Stop!" the officer's voice flashed. "You aren't allowed to leave."

Nozipho turned around. "Why not? It's all over."

"You can't. Orders. Why do you think everyone's standing around here?"

"Afraid of getting shot?"

"That, too..."

"But that's over."

"I'm sorry, but you have to wait until you have permission to move around the neighborhood. I'm waiting on word from the precinct."

"And if we just leave anyway?" Nozipho put her hands on her hips. Her dress tore a little more.

"Then...then..."

"We'll wait a few more minutes." Thembinkosi positioned himself so the world didn't have a view of Nozipho's underwear.

"Yes, I'm listening," the officer hollered into the mic. Silence, as they all tried to vainly listen in. "I understand," she finally said. "All right...Everyone now, and straight out. Got it."

Straight out sounds pretty good, Thembinkosi thought.

Before the officer could say another word, everyone started moving. The four garbage workers jammed themselves into the cab of their truck. The engine roared to life.

It wasn't much farther to the wall's ninety-degree corner. Leap, land safely, slow down. Look around. The crazy guy was still in sight, though he was hardly in a condition to follow him. The fire had already consumed a shrub.

New momentum. Over the wall, right leg up. Over the next one, child's play. Then a hedge and reduce speed. Turn to the right. One last glance back. The white man was standing there. Motionless. The fire had reached the branch of a tree. Speed up again. It couldn't be all that much farther.

It was getting harder for him to swing his legs over the obstacles. Again and again, and then he stopped. Four or five yards away from the one in which he was standing stood a tall wall that seemed to link the house to the outer wall. That was a good sign. He must be getting very close to the exit.

He carefully made his way to the last house. And discovered that his assumption had been on the mark. The connector between the houses and the outer wall ended here. Something was yelled on the other side of the wall. He could hear engine noise. That was the exit. All the curtains were pulled shut in this last house. It looked unoccupied. Leaves and dirt were scattered across the terrace. No threat should come from inside. He very slowly skirted the house to the street.

An entire convoy of police cars was just driving in. Small and large, a police van, then a prison transport vehicle with cells for arrested suspects. Moses ducked down and saw the exit. How long had it been since he had passed through there? He looked at his watch. 3:12. Over two hours ago.

Two Central Alert people, a man and a woman, were standing at the gate, along with two police officers, also a woman and a man. The gate swung open again for a black BMW with a mounted emergency flasher. Police top brass.

From the other direction, a gray compact car drew up. An old woman at the wheel. The policewoman stopped her with a wave. Opening the trunk, she looked inside. Thank you, keep driving. *Shit*, they had set up a checkpoint here.

The gate stayed open after the car drove off. Another convoy. Ambulances. All the private companies he had ever seen, one after the other. Had to be ten cars. An old Toyota bus was the last one to drive in. Scratched up, rusty, fumes belching from the exhaust pipe. All the first responders were needed here. Attenborough Ambulance was written on the side. Two of the letters were barely legible. He'd never heard of them.

How was he supposed to get out of here? Moses stared after the last ambulance, watched as it attached itself to the column. And for a split second, he thought he saw Sandi's face behind the wheel.

 "Come on," Nozipho said again. "We're leaving." She grabbed Thembinkosi's hand and took a step forward.

Everyone who had been standing around with them now started to move. The mail carrier checked his shoulder bag.

"Straight to the exit," the officer called once more.

"Aaaah," Thembinkosi said. "I thought for a second everything might get difficult." He wiped his forehead again, this time with his handkerchief.

"Give me that." Nozipho rubbed it over her forehead and lower arms, then under her arms, before handing it back. "We aren't out yet, you know."

One street up, a police convoy was crossing their path.

"But they aren't looking for us!"

"Not yet. But we don't know what's waiting for us at the exit."

 What would Sandi do?

She would look for him. Of course. So he just needed to stand somewhere where she could see him as she drove by. Only problem was that they'd probably catch him before she did that. Standing out somewhere wouldn't work.

What would?

Look for her himself. But then they might just keep missing each other, end up going down the wrong streets over and over again. They'd definitely catch him then.

At the end of the street, Moses caught sight of a garbage truck turning the corner. A couple of people were running behind the truck and throwing in the stuff sitting on the side of the road. And behind the truck, Moses briefly glimpsed the old ambulance. It didn't turn, but drove straight ahead. In the general direction from which he had just come. Sandi was looking for him.

Hide well enough that no one will see me. But such that I can see the street that Sandi will have to drive down. To see but not be seen. Moses looked around. A couple was now running around the corner that the garbage truck had just rounded. They dove for cover behind a small wall. *Strange,* he thought. But that wasn't his concern.

 "I don't know," Nozipho said as Thembinkosi came to a stop beside her. "Let's first see what's going on up there. Come on. The garbage truck will block us. Let's go!"

They ran along two front yards and stopped. "Look! They're running a checkpoint at the exit," Nozipho said. "Cops. Security."

"What should we do?"

"Be careful. Let's keep going."

She pulled Thembinkosi into a yard and knelt behind a hedge. He crouched next to her.

110 If she was proceeding methodically, she would have to come down this perimeter street that ran parallel to the wall.

Moses glanced around one more time. Less than a hundred meters from the exit. He crouched behind a garbage can

---

standing on the edge of the street. Checked it. Empty. The garbage truck had already been through here.

But where was the crazy man? He was the one Moses was scared of the most. He seemed determined, unscrupulous, and... well, crazy.

He could now see the garbage truck again. Very close to the exit. The workers were running back and forth throwing junk into the back. He had never seen garbage workers who ran. Maybe they wanted to get home.

Where was Sandi?

 "Up there. That's the last house, and those are the last bags they'll be throwing into the truck."

Nozipho hiked her dress high above her hips. She then grabbed Thembinkosi's hand. Grabbed it hard.

The three workers were tossing bags and cartons into the truck. Two of them vanished for a minute, reappearing with a can they emptied together. They looked at each other and flashed a thumbs-up signal. Done. Together they walked around the left side of the truck. The first man opened the door and hauled himself into the cab.

"Now!" Nozipho said.

The momentum of her sudden sprint took Thembinkosi by surprise. He stumbled forward in Nozipho's wake and dropped what he was carrying in his other hand. Pulled on her hand. In the other direction. They both almost came to a stop. But Nozipho was determined.

"The briefcase!"

"Doesn't matter. Come on!"

"But..."

"COME ON!" Nozipho shot him a toxic look.

Thembinkosi followed her. Together they ran after the truck as fast as they could.

An engine. Moses peered around the garbage can. Police. For a long moment, he became invisible. The vehicle drove by.

No white trash around. Another engine.

That. Was. The. Ambulance.

Sandi.

It slowly turned the corner. Moses glanced around. At the window behind him—the one right next to the front door of the house to which his trash can belonged—he caught sight of the nanny. The nanny who had helped him earlier. She was smiling at him. A raised thumb. Moses smiled back.

Sandi was still twenty meters away. *Wait one second,* he thought. *Wait one more.*

Still ten meters. Then only eight.

He leaped out from behind the trash can and stood on the street with outstretched arms. The vehicle screeched to a stop in front of him. Moses opened the passenger door and sat down. Breathed deeply. Wanted to hug Sandi.

"You have to get in the back!" she insisted, startling Moses.

"Go," she urged.

He squeezed between the seats into the back and was surprised to find a completely gutted space back there. There was nothing. A metal floor. Bare.

"Get down! We're leaving."

 Nozipho ran, Thembinkosi clinging to her hand.

The third worker was now climbing into the cab. The door was yanked shut.

Right before they reached the truck, Nozipho dropped his hand. She took a long stride and jumped onto the truck. Right onto the truck flap. Thembinkosi was too breathless to be astonished. Felt love. Felt disgust. Also jumped. Wasn't even hard to do. Wanted to be next to Nozipho.

He fell on top of her. Felt the air go out of her.

"Bury us under that stuff," she said.

The truck started moving. What a stench.

"That's garbage!"

"Bury us."

 The bus started moving but stopped almost right away.

"Check point at the exit. They're opening all the trunks." Moses didn't say anything.

"I think there are still three cars in front of us at the gate. Then a garbage truck. Phew...that reeks. And then us. Now the gate is opening. One car is leaving. Oh! There are people in the back of the garbage truck."

"What do you mean *people*?"

"People, as in people."

"In the garbage?"

"In the garbage."

"And?"

"They're hiding."

"In the garbage."

"In the garbage. We're down one more car."

"What kind of people?"

"How should I know? They're buried under the trash."

"White people?"

"The hand I just saw was black. One more car gone. Now they're at the garbage truck. They're looking in the cab. Someone is climbing up on the step. Back down again. And they're looking in the back. Now it's being waved through," she said. "We're up next."

For a second, nothing happened, but then he heard Sandi's voice. "Thank you, officer!"

Moses heard the gears shift. Second gear. Slowed down again. Turned. Drove. Away from here. What a nightmare.

 Meli was standing on the terrace behind Mrs. Viljoen's house. She had set a glass of juice on the plastic table and disappeared again.

"Stay here until it's over," she'd said. "Our lives aren't worth anything these days."

He could see her through the window on the phone and put his sunglasses back on. She didn't need to see him watching her. Otherwise he'd get another sermon. She hung up and came back out.

"You may leave now, even though it's only three o'clock. But you have to go straight to the exit. No detours. Understand? Those are the orders from the police."

"All right."

She handed him the hundred-rand bill he'd earned today and turned away. Before she closed the terrace door, she looked back one more time: "We live in terrible times. Next week, you'll have to make it work for real."

Meli had learned not to let the woman get to him. She was his oldest client. It had been almost five years since he'd started here. Once a week. She paid less than minimum wage, but she paid. At Christmas, there was a present for the children, usually something sweet, although she never asked about them. He didn't think she even knew he had three at home. Or how old they were.

He walked past the house, back to the street, and then turned left. Somewhere over there, the thing that had happened had happened. Of course, he'd go straight to the exit. Where else would he go? But he was curious. At the first intersection he reached, he had the option to turn left toward the exit. He decided differently. He wanted to know what had happened. People were coming out of their houses. An older woman in a bright apron and head cloth waved at him briefly.

Another intersection. The uniformed police officer standing there motioned him toward the exit. Meli stopped. A few meters on, another street branched off in the other direction. Yellow police tape. A privacy shield was being set up. Despite that, Meli could see the bodies. And the blood.

They all had to die eventually, he thought. What had happened to the boy with the afro? Meli wondered what had made him think of him. People were coming from all directions. The officer waved more energetically.

He'd seen enough. The others stopped, as he walked on.

The hundred rand would be enough for two days, then he had his job at the Aldersons. A half day. They'd insisted on that. A giant yard, but only a half day of work. *Better a half day than no day*, he'd told himself. He did as much work in those four hours as he did in a typical full day. And they had three cars.

He would stay home tomorrow. Liziwe would drive into the city. To the...he couldn't pronounce the name. And didn't know where they came from. But they weren't from here. He had to take care of the children tomorrow.

Two police cars were parked in front of a house. Two hearses, as well. Uniformed officers and some out of uniform. But you could still tell they were cops.

"Keep going. Keep going," one of the officers said.

Meli stopped.

"Keep going." The officer waved his arms.

The house looked like it had been in a war zone. Shot-out windows. Bullet holes everywhere.

"Keep going!" Louder now.

Two men walked out of the house carrying a stretcher. A white cloth over it, red spots on the white. Meli resumed his course. Everyone was fair game. Even the rich.

More police were coming from the other way. He counted them. Eight cars. If you needed help and called them from Duncan Village, they didn't send even one. He turned the hundred-rand bill over in his hand. Food and essentials, and if a little was left, a beer for him. Normally, there wasn't anything left.

Liziwe always looked at him so strangely whenever she caught a whiff of beer on him. They'd even argued about it once. Really argued. That hadn't been all that long ago.

"We don't even have enough money for the children, and you're always off drinking," she'd said.

Always, she'd said. She'd known that wasn't true. By the

next day, she was very nice to him.

Another convoy. Ambulances this time. Meli walked over to the side and leaned against a wall to wait. They sped off in the direction he'd just come from. The last one came to a stop in the middle of the intersection, though. For a second, it looked as if the driver wanted to ask him something. But then she turned.

A few steps further, and Meli could see the exit. And the cars that wanted to get out. A garbage truck blocked his view of part of the gate. He saw the guards and lots of police.

Lots of police was okay. Things only got dangerous when they were on their own or in pairs. One time, an officer had taken his day's earnings, simply because he could. Stopped him, searched him, money, money gone. Just like that. Meli hadn't even filed a complaint. What good would that have done?

Nobody here would steal his money. Too many eyes. Too much surveillance.

He could already smell the garbage truck. *They make more money than I do*, he thought. But he was very happy with his yards. Better to take care of the white people's yards than to haul off their trash. What a horrible smell. However, he also had a sensitive nose. And allergies for the past few years. You can't do anything about it, the doctor had said.

There was movement up on the garbage truck's flap. Meli rubbed his eyes. The truck rolled forward a little right then. *That's ridiculous,* he thought. Trash is trash, but he looked more closely at it. He almost didn't see the briefcase.

Brown leather, artificial leather actually. A little shimmer of gold at the handle. And big. Much larger than a typical briefcase.

Meli picked it up. It was heavy. Shook it.

Who'd leave a briefcase out here? Between a wall and a fynbos bush. He looked around. Nobody was watching him. Shook it one more time. There was something metallic inside. Clattered. But also something soft that absorbed the hard edges. *Had to be worthless, the contents*, he thought.

Otherwise, no one would have left it out here. Meli walked on.

By this point, the old ambulance had lined up behind the garbage truck. Would anyone want to look inside the briefcase?

A police officer was inspecting the trunk of a Hyundai. She closed it again, giving the driver a thumb's up. The gate opened. The Hyundai left The Pines. The gate was wide open. Two officers looked at him. Meli greeted them. They returned his greeting. He looked at the two security guards standing next to the cops and nodded politely. They nodded back in unison. He was out.

A short walk to the road to Abbotsford. A taxi was just speeding by. Every seat taken. He didn't want to pin his hopes on a taxi. Just figure you have to walk to Abbotsford. That would save him one rand in taxi fare. And he had no hope that someone would give him a lift to Abbotsford. The briefcase had to be worth a couple hundred rand. Maybe a thousand. He just needed to find someone who could pay that much. And first he needed to open it. He didn't want to break the lock. He'd figure it out.

The garbage truck passed him, stopping at the corner. Meli stared at the open cargo area again. There really was movement up there. He hadn't just dreamed it. Two people were climbing out of the garbage and scooting to the edge. At the very moment the truck accelerated, they jumped off. After tumbling to the ground, they quickly got to their feet and ran to the street. The woman in white tugged her dress over her thighs. The man in gray brushed off his suit. Where had he seen those two before? The woman stopped the man from dashing across the street. Autos sped by, and then they ran into the neighborhood across the way. He was sure he'd seen the two of them before.

The old ambulance pulled up and stopped next to him at the corner. The young woman at the wheel didn't look like someone who typically drove an ambulance. Shaved head. Tight t-shirt. Earring. He couldn't explain it, but for some reason, the woman didn't belong in there.

The ambulance turned toward Abbotsford. Maybe he should've tried to get a ride from her. He still had two kilometers to walk. Meli shook the briefcase again. He was quite curious to see what was inside.

A fire truck with flashing lights raced toward him. Meli watched after it and noticed that somewhere in the gated community, a fire was burning.

He walked on. What a strange day.

My thanks go to Anette Hoffmann, Dirk Lange and Yvonne Weissberg, who read my manuscript and provided feedback. Also, to Dorothee Plass and Martin Baltes who accompanied me during the writing process. To Gary Minkley for so very much. To Saskia Haardt for my image of myself. Last but not least, I am grateful to Paul Weller for "Brand New Day" and to Antje Schuhmann for Paul Weller.